Lucie Brandon

and the

Discovery of the Waya

To Jesse Kordenbrock!

Best Wishes!

Jennifer Dickson

Also by Jennifer Aiken Dickson

Lucie Brandon and the
Mystery of the Patchwork Dreams

Lucie Brandon and the Copper Mine Cache

Lucie Brandon

and the

Discovery of the Waya

Jennifer Aiken Dickson

ISBN-13: 978-1-7945-5598-3

To those who stand and speak

For the ones who have no voice

1

"Hey, can I borrow the hammer?" Andrea asked, reaching across the table.

"Let me finish this one," Lucie replied, and she proceeded to bang away at a particularly stubborn nail that was sticking out of the old wood. When it had been vanquished successfully, she slid the hammer in Andrea's direction and eyed her end of the table with satisfaction.

"How many more do you think are left?" Andrea asked in between hammer whacks on another nail. Her coppery-brown skin was shining as a result of their exertions, and she had her long black hair tucked into a knot on the back of her head to get it out of the way.

Lucie looked around at the booths that surrounded Shuford Lodge. "I think most of them have enough tables. This may be our last one. Maybe they'll put us on balloon detail next."

"Hey!" Lucie's brother Sean appeared around the corner of the woodcraft booth behind them, pushing a hand cart piled high with boxes. His brown hair was sticking up in all directions, and his slightly pointy ears were noticeable. "Take one of these for me, will ya?" he asked, rolling to a halt.

Lucie grabbed a heavy box off the top while Andrea took the next one. "Where are these going?" asked Andrea.

"They're supposed to be in the Honeydew Farms booth. Careful, they're full of jams and jellies," said Sean. "But the booth got relocated when the fried pies station needed more room, and these boxes got missed. You guys finished here?"

Lucie set her box on the repaired table and grabbed the hammer, lodging it in the belt of the carpenter's apron she was wearing over her shorts and t-shirt. "We are now," she announced, lifting the box again as the three set off down the aisle of booths.

"I'm coming back later to *that* booth," said Andrea, nodding at the candle carving booth. "They let you dip and carve your own," she said excitedly. "I'm going to do a red, white, and blue one."

Lucie blew upwards, trying to unstick her honey-brown bangs from her forehead. "I'm headed to the sno-cone truck soon. Boy, it sure is hot already!"

"It's early October in Georgia! The humid ain't gone yet!" laughed Andrea.

"Turn right at the quilt booth," said Sean, passing a flurry of color billowing out of a booth hung all over with scarves. The two twelve-year-old girls picked up the pace a little, ready to get in out of the sun. They saw the bright orange sign for Honeydew Farms halfway down the aisle on the left and homed in on it.

"There you are!" exclaimed a frizzy-haired, dumpy woman. She had a frown on her pale face. She was standing, hands on hips, behind the counter which was absolutely packed with jam, jelly, and honey jars.

"Where have you been?" she demanded as Sean rolled the handcart up over the bumpy grass.

Sean looked surprised. "Sorry, ma'am. Mr. Roderick had to take care of an emergency in the Lodge and gave me this cart five minutes ago."

"I needed these boxes half an hour ago!" she blustered, grabbing the one out of Lucie's arms and swinging it over the goods on the counter, setting it on the grass at the back of the booth. Her loose, mottled-purple blouse billowed out on each side, flapping under her arms like wings.

"Roll the cart back here and don't break any," she ordered Sean, reaching for Andrea's box next.

Sean did as she said, and as he began to unload the cart, she muscled him aside to set down Andrea's box, whipping her flyaway hair into his face in the process. "I'll get these," she snarled, lifting each box of the cart and finally shoving the handcart back at Sean. She then completely ignored the three kids, turning her back on them and leaning over double to examine the contents of the boxes.

Andrea and Lucie exchanged looks, then stepped away from the booth as they followed Sean and his handcart. When they were far enough away, the girls looked at each other again and then started giggling. Andrea gestured with her hands about her head, like she had big hair, and then flipped her arms around like a chicken.

Sean turned around and asked, "What's so funny?"

"That lady!" Andrea gasped. "She's just like one of my Aunt Bitsi's hens! All puffed up and pecking at anyone around her!"

"We were at Aunt Bitsi's house the other day, and she said that she'd never had a hen that cross before. And then she said," Lucie trailed off, turning to Andrea and starting to show signs of exploding in laughter again.

"You should see that chicken fly!" the girls chorused.

"And that lady's feathers certainly were ruffled!" gasped Andrea as the girls dissolved into another spasm of giggles.

Sean shook his head. "If she starts flying, I'm outa here."

He turned back to his handcart and pushed it down the grassy aisle, passing pottery and iron welding booths as well as one filled to the edges with doll clothes. The girls followed, ducking under some flags that roped off a shortcut alley to the main drive, which had a better surface for the handcart. They walked uphill and finally reached the front of Shuford Lodge which was the focal point for the day's arts and crafts Festival.

The Lodge itself was old. As it sat up on the hill, its foundations sunk into the red Georgia clay, it looked as if it had been there forever. The heavy beams under the floors had been hewn almost two hundred years ago, set into place by men and mules and determination. Its walls had settled long ago, some straight, some not so much.

Today, the autumn sun streaming on its fresh coat of yellow paint was a bright contrast to the deep brown of the shingles on the roof. Festive streamers reached from the porch columns to the limbs of the huge oaks that framed the front walkway, and balloons sprouted from the ground, attached to small stakes that sported celebratory flags. The Lodge was set for a wing-ding and a half.

They were met at the front by Mr. Roderick, the slim, pleasant man who was the curator of the Lodge. His deep tan set off by his dark hair, he was dressed comfortably for the hot day, but still managed to look professional in a blue short-sleeved button-down shirt and khakis.

"Looks like you found the Honeydew booth!" his pleasant voice greeted them as they approached. "Any problems?" he asked.

"Not if you don't pay attention to the chickens!" giggled Andrea, nudging Lucie with her shoulder, which set Lucie off again as well.

Sean gave her a look. "No, Mr. Roderick," he answered. "But the lady manning the Honeydew

Farms booth sure was ticked that she didn't have the boxes earlier."

"Yeah, you might say she was ready to fly right out of there!" Andrea said, her face full of merriment.

Mr. Roderick looked surprised. "Really? That's unfortunate. I'm sorry if it was uncomfortable. I'll be sure to check in with her later."

"Is there anything else we can help with, Mr. Roderick?" asked Lucie, pulling herself together.

Mr. Roderick's face brightened. "There is, actually, Lucie. All the balloons are in place for the front of the Lodge, and visitors will be arriving soon for the Festival. Will you and Andrea head into the Lodge and check in with Mrs. Martin? She's in the kitchen tallying the contributions for the baked goods booth. She just asked me to find some help for her. Sean, I've got a job for you over here, if you don't mind."

"No problem, Mr. Roderick," said Lucie. She and Andrea mounted the steps to the Lodge and went inside as Mr. Roderick led the way across the driveway, Sean following and fanning out his t-shirt to get some relief from the heat.

Inside the Lodge, the Art Show was on display, paintings hung on every wall. Sculptures stood throughout the rooms, on the floor, on pedestals, on shelves. Blown glass creations sparkled in the sunlight, while jewelry cases were lit tastefully to accentuate the necklaces, the earrings, the rings, and the bracelets within. Soft music played in the background.

Andrea was in the lead, weaving her way through the exhibits to the back of the house. As they passed through, they waved at Lucie's mom, Laurel, who was talking with a customer about the paintings she had created.

"Mrs. Martin?" Andrea called as they reached the back hallway.

"In here!" an elderly voice responded.

The girls found Mrs. Martin much as they had left the Honeydew Farms lady, doubled over looking at boxes on the floor. Mrs. Martin straightened her tall, willowy frame, her soft gray hair curled close to her head, and surveyed the girls.

"Just what the doctor ordered," she proclaimed. "I need someone to count cupcakes before my eyes start crossing!" She smiled at the girls and said, "Come here, you two!" and opened her arms wide. Andrea and Lucie giggled and rushed at her for a hug.

Andrea asked as she released them, "We can count, but are there any cupcakes that need to be, say, quality checked?" She grinned up at Mrs. Martin, raising one eyebrow.

"As I told you in my first-grade class," said Mrs. Martin, "quality checks are a must for cooks!" She reached behind her and produced two delectable-looking specimens, presenting them to the girls. "Consider them payment rendered for services about to be performed!" she proclaimed.

The girls peeled off the cupcake wrappers and sank their teeth into the moist, fluffy treats. "Did you make your famous peach cobbler this year, Mrs. Martin?" asked Lucie around a mouthful of cake.

"Of course I did!" said Mrs. Martin. "But it's my pecan pie that I'm most excited to share. It has special pecans this time, from my cousin in Kentucky. She always brings some down when she visits, but this time I remembered to save some for the Festival. I've entered it in the pie contest."

"You don't use South Georgia pecans, Mrs. Martin?" Andrea asked.

"I usually do, Andrea, but these are something special. Maybe it's just the fact that they come from a family orchard, but I do love the taste," answered Mrs. Martin. "Now, if the two of you have finished your snack, why don't you wash your hands, and we'll get to work?"

The girls willingly moved to the big farm sink. Lucie untied and rolled up her carpenter's apron while Andrea licked the stray purple frosting from her fingers, and then they twisted the taps and plunged their hands into the water. Having scrubbed thoroughly, they fell into working with Mrs. Martin, cataloguing the various cakes, pies, and pastries first, then ferrying them out through the day to the baked goods booth, as it had little safe storage room on its plot. In between deliveries they had some free time to dart around the Festival and visit some favorite booths.

The Festival got very crowded, with people strolling and shopping, filling up the aisles between the booths. Whimsical and practical pottery, bread, quilts, cookies, fried pies, home-gathered honey, boiled peanuts, sorghum syrup, delicate jewelry, artful iron welding, framed photographs, carved wooden ornaments, baskets… all and more were on display.

They wound their way behind the Lodge to the cornhole toss and the bow-and-arrow competition and followed rousing music to the barn, where the dance exhibitions were staged. The river at the base of the hill was festooned with brightly-colored flags, and picnics dotted its banks as families stopped to rest and refuel. Andrea and Lucie met up with some friends from school and had a race through the corn maze, only getting lost two or three times, dissolving into giggles as they bumbled their way through.

It was late in the afternoon when the storm clouds started rolling in, darkening the skies and threatening to put a serious damper on the celebration. Visitors were gathering children and packages, streaming away down the hill to their cars. Lucie and Andrea were back in the kitchen, helping Mrs. Martin to pack up the remaining baked goods to be taken as donations to the Hoxit Community Food Pantry. Mrs. Martin was having trouble fitting the items into the boxes she'd brought from home, and she was getting frustrated.

"Girls, can you pop downstairs to the basement storage room and see if you can snag some extra boxes?" she asked.

"Yepper-doodle," Andrea said lightly, and Lucie followed her reluctantly down the rear staircase. Andrea flipped on the light switch at the bottom of the stairs and saw Lucie shudder slightly.

"Hey, what's up?" she asked Lucie.

"I dunno. I always get uneasy inside this Lodge. I just got a chill run across my back. It's just... Can we get the boxes and get out of here?" Lucie said as she started with Andrea across the worn stone floor.

Andrea gave her a concerned look and said, "Are you sure? It is kind of spooky down here."

"Yeah. Hey, watch out for that big crack in the floor!" Lucie pulled Andrea back just as she started to trip. Lightning flashed outside.

"Hey, thanks." Andrea stepped over the uneven stones. "What about this room?" she asked, reaching for the door knob to check inside.

Just then, there was a huge clap of thunder, and they were plunged into darkness.

"What just happened?" wondered Lucie.

"Must be the storm," decided Andrea. "Those clouds sure came in fast. I can't see anything, can you?"

"No, but there are windows in some of the rooms," answered Lucie. "If we can get a door open, we may get some light to find our way out. I wonder why we can't see the stairs?"

"That door up at the top opens into the hallway—maybe somebody closed it as they went by? Lots of people are packing up to go home," mused Andrea. She rattled the doorknob. "This door is locked. Let's feel our way to another one."

Lucie ran her hand along the wall, trying to find another door. The next one was locked, and the next, but the third she tried opened easily at her touch. "Here!" she cried back to Andrea.

As she felt her way into the room, a blazing flash of lightning burst through the rectangular window facing Lucie, followed immediately by another enormous boom of thunder that shook the building.

In that flash she saw a hundred faces: angry, smiling, grotesque, beseeching, all around the walls from the floor to the ceiling. As she reeled back from the cacophony of images, she felt a strong hand grab her shoulder—and Lucie screamed!!

2

In one ear, Lucie heard another scream, and she screamed again, competing with crashes of thunder outside. The hand on her shoulder jerked, and Lucie whipped around to see Andrea, eyes wide, looking terrified. Then they both seemed to come to their senses at the same time, just as another flash of lightning came through the window. The faces flashed around them again, as did the sequined heart on Andrea's shirt, and they heard pounding feet on the stairs.

"Girls!" shouted a man's voice.

"Lucie? Andrea?" called a woman.

A beam of light zoomed into the basement, bouncing here and there. The girls looked out of the doorway to be blinded by the flashlight.

"Are you okay?" asked Mrs. Martin's voice. "We heard you scream!"

The man in front of her rushed off the stairs toward the girls. They heard an "Ooof!!" and saw the flashlight go flying as something heavy hit the floor.

"Ken!" cried Mrs. Martin.

Just then the electricity bloomed on, and the basement was flooded with light. Blinking in the sudden brightness, Lucie and Andrea saw Mr. Roderick sprawled flat on his stomach across the stones of the basement floor.

"Mr. Roderick!" cried Lucie, and the girls rushed forward to help him up. Mr. Roderick ruefully brushed himself off, and Andrea found the flashlight shining in a corner and retrieved it, handing it back to him.

"That happens almost every time I come down here," said Mr. Roderick, shaking his head. "You'd think I'd get a clue and do something about it."

"What's all this fuss?" another man's voice floated down the stairs. Mrs. Martin turned to see who was speaking.

"Emmett Prendergast! I didn't know you were here today!" she said.

"Well, I am, and I've asked a question, Mamie! What is all this infernal din?" the crusty, ruddy-cheeked man demanded as he creaked his way down the stairs, his cane thumping on each step.

"I'm sorry. I got startled, with the lightning and thunder and all, and then Mr. Roderick tripped on this big crack in the floor," volunteered Lucie. "Are you okay, Mr. Roderick?"

"Oh, yes, I'm fine. I think my pride is hurt more than anything," he told her, smiling ruefully.

"But more importantly, why were you screaming? Are either of you hurt?"

Lucie's light skin turned a little pink from embarrassment. "We were looking for boxes for Mrs. Martin, and the electricity went out, and then I opened that door there. I saw all sorts of faces in the lightning flash, and they startled me! Andrea caught my shoulder and that surprised me too! I'm sorry I made such a ruckus."

"Faces?" barked Mr. Prendergast. "There are other people down here?" He looked around.

"No," replied Lucie. "But they were surrounding me, and they had all kinds of gruesome expressions."

"Ah! I know what you've found!" Mr. Roderick laughed a little and laid a hand on her shoulder. "You've found the face jugs room."

"Face jugs?" asked Andrea, wrinkling up her own face.

"Sure, come on in here," invited Mr. Roderick. He led the group back into the room from which Lucie and Andrea had emerged, flipping on the light switch for good measure. Shelves lined the walls, and from floor to ceiling were pottery jugs, many of them dark green or black, and every one of them possessed a face. Some were comical, some were gruesome, and some were just downright ugly.

"I didn't remember that the Lodge had such a collection of face jugs!" Mrs. Martin marveled. "No wonder you girls were startled. If you aren't used to the face jugs phenomenon, it can sure give a body a turn."

"Face jugs aren't original to North Georgia, you know," said Mr. Prendergast imperiously, "even though they are quite prevalent here now."

"I thought they started here," exclaimed Mrs. Martin. "The Meaders family certainly made them famous."

"Yes, yes, Lanier Meaders's getting some of his work in the Smithsonian American Art Museum did boost attention to them," gruffed Mr. Prendergast, leaning heavily on his cane. "But they actually started in South Carolina. Slaves were making them, slaves that were from Kongo societies of Western Africa. Some believe that the face jugs were designed in their culture for use in a ceremony to contact the spirit world. Others speculate that the faces were a warning that the contents were dangerous."

"Slaves made these first?" asked Andrea, reaching out to touch one gently.

"Yes, and then the North Georgia potters continued the art," said Mr. Prendergast. "You should see some of the art shows over in Sautee-Nacoochee. Face jugs of all kinds. They have a folk pottery museum up there, as well as an old slave cabin that's been restored. I must say," he mused condescendingly, looking around the room, "this collection is actually quite impressive, Roderick."

"Thank you, Emmett," said Mr. Roderick, seeming to smother an amused smile at Mr.

Prendergast's pompous tone. "It's the next big exhibit for the Kenimer room upstairs. We'll be putting them in place once we clean up from this event."

The group started to file out of the room, and as the adults mounted the stairs, Lucie hung back a little, looking at the different faces and glazes on the jugs. Her mother was an artist and often worked with clay. Lucie had seen face jugs before at art shows with her mother, so she wondered why these had terrified her so.

Andrea popped her head back in the doorway. "Hey, you comin'? I've got boxes to take upstairs."

"Yeah," said Lucie, leaving the room and taking a few boxes from Andrea's arms. Andrea forgot about the uneven floor, however, and the next thing they knew, she was falling and sprawled out on the basement floor, her sneaker stubbed on the big crack, the boxes strewn in front of her.

"Ooof!!" All the air went out of Andrea, and she lay there for a moment on her stomach.

"Are you okay?" asked Lucie, concerned.

"Yeah," said Andrea. "That stupid crack! I can't believe I stubbed my toe on... Wait a minute, Luce," she continued slowly.

"What?" asked Lucie.

"Look at this!" Andrea said, propping herself up on her elbows and pointing to part of the stone floor right in front of where her nose had been. Lucie put her boxes down and crouched beside Andrea. "You mean this stone triangle?" Lucie asked.

"Yeah! It looks like an arrowhead, doesn't it?" said Andrea.

"Well, now that you mention it, yeah, it does," replied Lucie. "Wonder how it got in the floor?"

Andrea sat up and leaned over the arrowhead, tracing the outline to the point. "I don't know. Here, feel it. It's really smooth. Arrowheads are usually bumpier than this."

Lucie reached out to touch the arrowhead, and as soon as she made contact, she drew back quickly with a "YOW!" Her hazel eyes were as big as saucers.

"What is it?" Andrea exclaimed.

"Oh, man, here we go again!" Lucie said, shaking her head.

"Wait, what? Did you get an ancestor zap?" asked Andrea, getting excited.

"Like you wouldn't believe," Lucie replied, looking at Andrea. "This is just the weirdest day. First that lady getting all grumpy and fussing, then the thunderstorm and the face jugs startling me, and now an arrowhead that zaps me!"

Andrea's face was lit up with glee. "This is great!" she said, getting to her feet and pulling the tumbled boxes into her arms. "We haven't had a mystery in months! And it'll be a great change from homework!"

Lucie picked up her own boxes and headed up the stairs. "Yeah, but we'll need a lot more to go on before we know where this is headed."

Andrea trudged up the stairs behind her, looking back halfway up and flashing a frown at the crack in the floor. "What's that word Ms. Brockworth uses in language arts when she wants us to be more forceful?"

"Emphatic?"

"Yeah. Emphatic. If the ancestors could be a little less *emphatic* when they try to get our attention, my nose and knees would thank them, emphatically!" Andrea laughed as she and Lucie cleared the top of the stairs and started toward their next adventure.

3

Lucie flopped into a squashy armchair in the living room, her hair wet from her shower. She was exhausted from the long day, in and out of the sun. Sean was lying on the couch watching football on TV, and he looked as zonked as she felt. Their basset hound, Carson, was stretched out on the floor, snoring gently.

"Ready for bed, sweetie?" their mom, Laurel, asked from the corner of the room where she was curled up on a loveseat beside her husband, doing a crossword puzzle on her tablet.

"Yeah," replied Lucie. "You were right; the shower really felt good."

"Sometimes that's all a body needs," said her dad, Rob. He was watching the Georgia-Auburn game, too, munching on popcorn with his feet up.

He turned his attention to Lucie, however. "You think your ancestor dream will come tonight?" he asked.

This past summer, Lucie had discovered that she possessed a special gift. She and Andrea had solved two mysteries, aided by incredibly vivid dreams that came to Lucie from her ancestors. In the dreams, she saw a day in their lives, and somewhere within each of the dreams would be a clue that guided Andrea and Lucie in their sleuthing. Very often, Lucie felt an electric tingle, just like the zap she had felt earlier that evening in the Shuford Lodge basement, and that was a sure sign that a dream was on its way.

She had told her family about the strange events in the Shuford Lodge basement on their way home from the Festival, and they were all anticipating an exciting few weeks as the next mystery unfolded.

Lucie responded, "I bet it will. I just hope I can follow it. I'm so tired!" She rested her head on the back of the chair and gazed at the television with heavy eyes.

"You both did good work, lending a hand at the Festival," Laurel told them. "I don't think I left the Art Gallery display all day, but every now and then I'd see you pass by."

"Mom, who was… Whoa, did you see that, Dad?" Sean yelled, his eyes glued to the television. "That was totally pass interference! How did they miss it?"

"Wait for the replay. The coaches are making some noise," replied Rob. "They have to have clear evidence to overturn the call." He popped some more popcorn in his mouth and munched away.

Laurel was looking at her son. "Sean, you were asking something?"

Sean tore his eyes away from the screen momentarily, his expression blank, and then he remembered. "Yeah, Mom, do you know who was manning the Honeydew Farms booth?"

"Wasn't Carmen Littlegalle down for that?" Laurel responded. "She usually sends someone else to the Festival, though. Why do you ask?"

Sean was yelling at the TV again. "See, Dad? He didn't even turn to look at the ball!"

Laurel looked at Lucie, amused. "Was it something I said?" she asked.

Lucie giggled. "Nah. But Carmen Littlegalle sure said stuff. She was in an ill mood when we brought some of her supplies down to her booth, and she reminded Andrea and me of a wet hen, all puffed up and clucking and bumping Sean aside with her rear end."

Laurel frowned. "But Carmen has always been so pleasant to me…" Her voice trailed off, a puzzled look on her face, her hand reaching up to push a honey-brown lock of hair, so like Lucie's own, behind her ear.

"Yes! Touchdown!" Sean shouted, shooting his arms up in the air and awakening Carson.

Lucie shook her weary head. "I think I'd better go to bed. This is too much excitement for me!"

She got up out of the chair and went over to her parents, giving them each a kiss on the cheek good night. "Sweet dreams," her mother told her, and Lucie gave her an extra smile. She left the living room and went down the hallway to her own pretty, shell-pink bedroom, followed closely by Carson. He took a huge running leap to jump on her bed, turned around three times, and then collapsed with satisfaction on the fleece blanket at the foot of her bed, eyeing her sideways to make sure she wasn't going to boot him off.

Lucie climbed into her cool, mint green sheets and pulled her summer quilt over herself. She stretched an arm out to turn off her bedside lamp and then lay her head on her soft, comfortable pillow. Almost immediately, she was swept off into dreamland, her ancestors whisking her away to another distant night.

Ballard County, Kentucky
August 1870

The music floated on the air, beautiful and plaintive. The tall, slender man had the violin tucked under his closely bearded chin, and his dark hair was kissed by the sweet breeze coming across the fields from the Mississippi River, meandering its way across the wide front porch. His thin face was concentrated on his instrument, drawing the bow lovingly across the strings, making the notes sing achingly before he released them and began the next phrase.

The children were playing tag in the grass, the two older boys encouraging the toddler to catch them, calling, "Come on, Bob!" He giggled, chasing them with his arms held wide and his little feet churning as fast as they could go. Every so often he would tumble to the ground, and the big boys would laugh and roll down into the grass with him, tickling him and then springing to their feet to begin again.

She sat in a rocking chair on the porch, her pregnant belly very evident under her long dress. Her feet rested on a footstool, and she was grateful for the help, as her ankles were quite swollen this late in her pregnancy. She rocked, reveling in the beauty of the moment after a long day of housework and wrangling children as she rested her head on the back of the chair, watching her husband.

He brought the song to a sweet, heart-stopping end and stood there in the moment, waiting as the last remnants of sound disappeared. Then he turned and smiled at his young wife, and she smiled back.

"What was that, love?" she asked.

"It's an old riddle song, *I gave my love an apple*," said he. He sang the words for her:

"I will give my love an apple without any core
I will give my love a house without any door
I will give my love a palace wherein she may be
And she may unlock it without any key.

My head is the apple without any core
My mind is the house without any door
My heart is the palace wherein she may be
And she may unlock it without any key."

"It makes me think of you, and your generosity, and how you have embraced our whole family with your love," he told her.

She was suddenly shy. "Oh, Masterson, Eva would have wanted it. And Charlie and William have been lovely, even though they miss their real Ma dreadfully at times."

"You are their Ma now, George Ann," he said gently. "Eva thought quite highly of you; you know that. We will always mourn her, but we celebrate her through those good boys."

George Ann continued to rock gently, gazing at the boys who were now trying to catch lightning bugs. "Bob is going to be exhausted, running after the big boys," she said.

"He will sleep well tonight!" Masterson smiled. "Perhaps he will even sleep the night through!"

Her eyes met his in laughter at such an improbable event. "Ah, well, I will be up with this one sometime in the night anyway," she said, gesturing to the babe in her swollen belly. "I can't seem to stay comfortable for long these days."

He came to sit beside her in a straight chair, resting his violin on his lap.

"How was your day?" she asked, reaching out to touch his arm. "You came to supper right as I was getting the boys to the table, and there wasn't an opportunity to ask."

"It went well," replied Masterson. "I saw several patients with summer colds in the morning, and I went in the buggy this afternoon to see others. I was late getting home because I think I have finally convinced Thom McGruder to allow his wife to have surgery."

"Oh! I can't believe it!" exclaimed George Ann. "How did you do it?"

"She needs it so badly," said Masterson, shaking his head. "Patience McGruder will have to travel to Paducah for the procedure, but she will not survive without it, and so she must go. I had a word about the seriousness of the situation last week with Thom's son Patrick and his wife Katrine. Between the two of them, they worked on the old man for days, as well as bringing in a few of his trusted cronies to help, and that seems to have done it."

George Ann gazed gratefully, admiringly at this man who was her husband. "So, the message finally got through," she said with satisfaction. "You just had to find the right ear to listen."

"And not before time," he replied. "Time's a wastin', and we must preserve what we can. Enjoy while we can, for we never know what is beyond the bend in the road." He put his hand over hers on the arm of the rocking chair and held it gently in his.

They sat in the gathering dusk, watching the children in the yard and the emerging stars in the deep blue sky, until he shook himself and said, "How about one more before bed?" He picked up his violin and called to the boys, "How about *The Paw Paw Patch*, fellows?"

The boys whooped and ran towards each other, grabbing hands to make a circle as their father's violin lit into the rollicking, joyous tune. They danced and sang "*way down yonder in the paw paw patch*" and picked up the invisible paw paws, putting them in their imaginary baskets, and teaching their little brother as they went.

George Ann clapped her hands and laughed, suffused with uncomplicated joy.

Lucie turned over in bed, briefly waking, and looked up into the skylight over her bed. The dark sky was covered in stars, just like in her dream, and before her eyes drifted back into sleep, one star seemed to flash brighter than the others. Lucie smiled and snuggled back into her cozy nest, Carson snoring at her feet.

4

On Monday, Lucie dragged a music stand from the stand carrier and took it to her chair, where she had already carefully placed her Horn. She put her music on the stand, picked up her Horn, and then sat down, avoiding Tristan Phelps as he bulldozed his way through the set with his own stand, narrowly missing thwacking her in the head with it. He plunked the stand down in the row in front of Lucie, and then departed, presumably to go get his bass clarinet.

"BRawww-eee-bopp!" Lucie jumped as she was bombarded with brassy trombone. She turned around.

"Kelton! Leave my friend alone!" demanded Andrea, arriving with her own trombone just as Kelton was pelting Lucie with sound.

"Brrrapppp!" was his musical response, but he did move away and sat a few seats down the row, pushing back his long, ash-brown hair and grinning at Lucie.

"Mrs. Brackley!" Cynthia Jones called from the second row to the director's stand. "I left my music in my locker. Can I go get it?"

"That's the third time in a week, Cynthia," said their band director wearily. She'd come by her silver-streaked hair honestly, from years of being patient with teenagers. "As a seventh grader, you should…" Her sentence was gradually drowned out by the growing noises of students moving equipment and warming up their instruments.

Amy Lucas sat down primly in the row in front of Lucie. She opened her oboe case on her lap and immediately popped her reed into the side of her mouth. As she began putting her oboe together, she swiveled sideways to talk to Lucie, keeping her knees away from Tristan, who had returned.

"Hey, Lucie!" she greeted her. "Did you get that social studies project done?"

"Yeah, but I stayed up late last night to do it," said Lucie, looking tired. "I submitted it in the drop box before I went to bed."

"My internet at home kept going out, and it took forever to get all the pictures in my presentation," said Amy, rolling her eyes.

"I finished mine last week," interjected Andrea, whose attention had been captured. "Which is good, because I was gone all weekend, first with the Festival and then at my Grandma's in Hiawassee yesterday."

Lucie shifted in her chair to look back at Andrea. "Hey, I have to tell you something!"

The conversation was stopped by Mrs.

Brackley holding up her hands for silence. "Good morning!" she greeted her band students. "We have several announcements before we get going today… Yes, Emily?" looking at the strawberry-blonde, curly-haired girl beside Andrea whose hand was waving in the air.

Emily Carter lowered her hand. "Mrs. Brackley, do you have a school trombone I can borrow?"

Lucie turned to look, and sure enough, Emily was trombone-less.

"I may have one," Mrs. Brackley looked vaguely toward the instrument lockers. "But what happened to yours, Emily? You don't usually forget your instrument."

"Well, you see," began Emily, "I took my trombone out of the trunk of the car yesterday afternoon while I was helping my mom unload groceries, and then we noticed my dog was acting funny, and then he got sick on the living room carpet."

The boys were making gagging motions farther down the low-brass row.

"And then my little brother dumped all his Legos in the hallway outside his room, and I stepped on them in my bare feet, because I'd taken off my flip-flops, and there was a lot of screaming."

Amy was not the only student who winced at the image.

"Then my mom realized she was late picking my sister up from basketball practice, and she rushed out of the house to get her and almost forgot to take her keys and her purse, which actually in the end would have been a better thing to forget her keys, but not her purse in case she was in an accident or something," Emily concluded.

By this time, the whole class was riveted, but a little confused. So was Mrs. Brackley. "Emily, I'm sorry," she said, rubbing her forehead. "But what does this have to do with your trombone?"

"I never got my trombone from behind the car, and my mom ran over it, *ka-thunk ka-thunk!*, as she raced out of the driveway! It's flat as a pancake! I've got pictures, see?" Emily held up her phone, and the class completely erupted in mirth.

Emily passed her phone to Lucie, who after peeking at the photo gave it to Amy, who (peeking) passed it into the flute section, who (group goggling) got it to Mrs. Brackley. Emily looked very earnest and innocent in her seat, but Andrea had her head back, suffused in giggles, hugging her own trombone to her as she held her sides as if they would split, tears running down her cheeks.

"Yep, that's flat alright," was Mrs. Brackley's verdict, which sent the class into further spasms. "Emily, look in that last locker by the door. I think there's a spare trombone in there. Look for one that has a yellow tag on it."

As Emily went to look, Mrs. Brackley turned her attention to the rest of her seventh-grade class, waiting until their mirth was spent. She pushed back the sleeves on her navy-blue shirt and waited expectantly. When they were settled, she spoke.

"Thank you to those of you who turned in recordings of your pass-off lines. I've listened to them and updated the chart; you can double-check me at the end of class. Don't forget that District Band auditions are coming up soon, and those of you who are interested need to start working up your scales and etudes. Don't leave them until the last minute!" She gave her class a stern look with narrowed eyes, and then she smiled. "I'll be here after school all this week if anyone needs any help or wants to practice sight-reading."

She picked up a stack of papers from her music stand, stepped down from the podium, and started sending pages down each row while she explained.

"This is a permission form for the Band Spirit Night at the McCall-Stephens County football game two Fridays from now. The eighth-grade band members have been invited to play along with the high school marching band in the stands, but you will have to wait until next year for that pleasure. You are, however, invited to attend as the guests of the high school band to augment their cheering section, and if you attend you will receive a band t-shirt as well as free pizza!"

Moderate excitement rippled across the room. She continued, "If you are interested in participating, have a parent complete this form and return it to me by this Friday. Any questions?"

Tristan had his hand raised. "Mrs. Brackley, I want to attend, but I'm lactose intolerant, and I can't eat pizza with cheese." The freckles on his face seemed to stand out in his concern, and his ears were almost as red as his hair with self-consciousness.

Mrs. Brackley said smoothly, "Tristan, I'm sure we can find a substitute for you that night."

Reassured, Tristan looked back down at his flyer and started to read it through.

"The bands from both high schools will be performing their contest shows that night," said Mrs. Brackley, "and you will have a wonderful view of both. I highly encourage all of you to attend if you can, because both bands have very exciting shows this year."

She looked at the white board to see if she had forgotten anything, and then turned back to her class. "Okay! Looks like it's time to get started. Concert Bb scale, and then we'll do a chorale." Stepping onto her podium, she raised her arms and, when she had everyone ready to play, began to guide them once more through the world of music.

In social studies later that afternoon, Amy proudly held up her hands to frame the final slide of her presentation. "And that's how my family tamed the wilds of Northeast Georgia in the early 1800s!" she finished triumphantly.

The class clapped dutifully, and Mr. Kishpaugh stood up. His curly chestnut hair accented his big, teddy-bear appearance and made him very popular with the students. "Good job, Amy," he said, checking the clock. "We'll hold off further presentations until tomorrow. Now, you have an extra credit opportunity, should you choose to accept it."

He pointed at the white board. "I've written several locations, with websites, upon the board. Some of them have been mentioned in your presentations today as well as in other classes as having significant meaning to your families. All of them have some connection to the historical development of McCall County, such as the DeJournett House, the Crack-Stackin' Pottery, and Smokey Creek. Not all on the list are in McCall County, but each one has some influence on this area of Northeast Georgia. Can you think of any other sites like these?"

Andrea raised her hand. "My dad has taken us up to Track Rock Gap in Union County to see the soapstone rocks. People carved images in them thousands of years ago."

Tristan piped up from beside the window, "There's another rock like that in Western North Carolina, too, near Cullowhee. It's called Judaculla, and the carvings are called petroglyphs. I've heard ghost stories about it, and loads of people visit it every year. The carvings are two to three thousand years old."

"People were here thousands of years ago?" Lily Jenks was skeptical.

"There is evidence that Native Americans lived in the North Georgia area ten thousand years ago," confirmed Mr. Kishpaugh. "They and later civilizations shaped this land significantly. Does anyone know of other evidence they left?"

Tommy Nelis pushed up his glasses and raised his hand. "My granddad lives in Walhalla, South Carolina, and he always talks about the Cherokee canoe they pulled out of the Chattooga River. One of his friends was part of the team that walked it up the river to get it out. They had to use a crane and a truck to move it, and it's in the Oconee Heritage Museum now, with another one they found later. They're preserved and everything."

"Excellent, all," said Mr. Kishpaugh, adding the three locations to the white board. "These are exactly the kind of experiences we're looking for. Your extra credit assignment is to visit one of these sites, or another one approved by me, by next Monday. Complete a summary of your visit, include a picture of you visiting the site, and submit it electronically to the school homework portal. You do have to physically visit the site," he grinned, as soft groans were audible from the back of the room, "not just research online! And no digital editing yourself in!"

He pulled up the assignment on the school homework portal and projected it onto the screen. "Check the availability of tours before you make any decisions. Some places, like the Crack-Stackin'

Pottery, only give tours on Wednesdays and Saturdays. So, plan ahead!" he said. "Any questions?"

Before anyone could get overzealous and think of one, the bell rang for class to end, and the students started gathering belongings. Andrea and Lucie left the room together, talking about the assignment.

"I've already been to the petroglyphs sites, and we went to the DeJournett House in Junius this summer," said Andrea.

"I can't do anything Saturday," said Lucie. "That's when Nana and Gran are holding the quilting party for my birthday ancestor quilt."

The girls scooted through a gap in the crowd, and then Andrea turned to Lucie. "I'll check with my mom," she said. "I think the Terrible Twins have gymnastics on Thursday, so that's out too." She bumped into a girl getting something out of a bottom locker. "Oh! Sorry!" she told her. "Hey, you said in band you had something to tell me?" she asked Lucie.

"I had a…" Lucie started, but then Andrea jumped again. "I missed my class!" she cried, and she turned around and headed for a nearby doorway, her dark hair flying behind her. "Tell me later!"

"See you!" Lucie called, and she hurried toward the stairwell leading to her next class.

5

After school, Lucie got off the bus at Nana and Pop's house and crunched down the gravel driveway, crossing the wooden bridge over the stream that meandered in front of the house. She was hailed from the front porch as she reached the front yard.

"Lucie! Come to the front, pet!" called Nana.

Lucie made her way along the stone footpath to the front steps of the two-story, white-clapboard Victorian. The generous front porch was supported by slender double columns, and the emerald green shutters on either side of the windows gave a crisp, classic finish to the house.

Nan Stafford, Lucie's Nana, and her mother, Patsy Culwen, Lucie's Gran, were sitting in two of the rocking chairs that were scattered along the length of the porch, which was decorated with pumpkins and harvest decorations. Nana was in fine form today, resplendent in jeans and a sweatshirt covered in a riot of fall leaves that clashed with her vivid hair, and Gran, much more quietly dressed in pastels, looked like she'd drifted off for a nap.

"Come take a load off!" invited Nana as she put down the quilting square she was piecing and held her arms out for a hug.

Gran's eyes fluttered open and came into focus on Lucie as she hugged Nana. "Been snoozing, Gran?" asked Lucie as she gave her a quick hug.

"Not snoozing!" denied Gran indignantly, smoothing back her silver hair. "Just resting my eyes a bit." She rustled the newspaper in her lap to emphasize her point.

Lucie grinned and, dumping her backpack on the porch, said, "I'll grab a snack and be back out." She opened the screened door and was immediately strafed by a red-and-cream blur of fluff. "Rotunda!" Lucie giggled, and she dropped to the floor. The Persian kitten raced into the living room, zoomed around the coffee table in front of the navy couch, and then stopped, tail swishing, feet splayed, to face Lucie.

"You are a very fast girl!" Lucie told her, and she wiggled her hand in front of her. Rotunda's amber eyes watched Lucie's hand as she considered her options, and then she plunged forward to tag Lucie's hand. Lucie quick as a wink ran her hand along Rotunda's silky red back, feeling her solid, round body under the beautiful fur. Rotunda stopped in mid-scoot and came back for more, arching her back against Lucie's caresses. Lucie finally picked her up, cuddling the kitten against her chest, and walked on through the house into the kitchen, where she grabbed a water and some grapes from the fridge.

Taking her catch back to the front porch, she settled into the big porch swing, arranging the pillows so she could lean back and stretch her legs longways.

"You look tired, Lucie," observed Gran, as Lucie released Rotunda, who stomped around on Lucie's stomach for a bit before curling up on her lap, burying her snub nose in her fluffy tail while her amber eyes peeped above, still watchful.

"I stayed up late finishing that family project for Social Studies," explained Lucie, opening her water and taking a drink. "I thought I'd never get it done." She popped a grape into her mouth and crunched into the sweetness.

"We were so excited yesterday when you called about having another ancestor dream," Nana told her. "The name Masterson was an obvious clue; the Hawthornes are my dad's people, and we checked Gran's records for the time period of your dream. George Ann's baby was born right after the 1870 census was taken, and it was just months after that, in December, when Dr. Masterson Hawthorne passed away. And then George Ann disappears from the records before 1880."

"She disappears?" Lucie was stricken.

"The children were living with George Ann's parents in the 1880 census, and George Ann isn't there. Records in Ballard County, where they lived, were largely destroyed by a fire in 1880, so we haven't been able to find a record of George Ann's death," explained Gran.

"They looked so happy, Nana," said Lucie sadly. "The whole family was full of joy."

"I'm so glad you got to see them that way," said Nana gently. "Being remembered with love is perhaps the best tribute to them we can give."

Rotunda's little claws tensed on Lucie's jeans for a minute as she felt Lucie's sadness, and then she relaxed, cuddling into Lucie and butting her head against Lucie's hand. Lucie automatically began to pet her, stroking the warm little body, and Rotunda's distinctive, throaty purr began to rumble. Lucie finished her snack, put her water bottle on the floor, and leaned against her pillows, rocking a little in the big swing. She kept massaging Rotunda's back, listening to her grandmothers' quiet chatter. The combination of soothing motion, warm kitten, and late-night-homework made it very easy for her eyelids to become heavier and heavier, until finally she gave in and closed her eyes, sinking into dream.

Fairfield District, South Carolina 1795

The tall man was shouting. He was shouting at her friends, and they looked scared. They stood in a line, the sweat dripping down their bodies from the sweltering South Carolina afternoon. Their dark faces turned away from him, trying to get away somehow, even though their feet were not allowed to move.

"I am in charge here! I am the Overseer! You will do as I say, or I will go to Mr. Cameron and tell him of your laziness. Do you wish me to fetch the whip?"

He strode in front of the small group in his shining, knee-high boots, hands on his narrow hips, and then motioned to the heaping baskets of cotton lined up on the barn floor.

"Faster, I say! This day's harvest is unacceptable. You must pick more! You will go back out after dinner to make up the difference. I do not care if your fingers are bloodied, or your skin burns from the sun. Am I understood?" he demanded.

He puffed out his chest and jutted his bearded chin forward to look more important. "Mr. Cameron has plans to expand, to add more workers, to make this farm a jewel in the South Carolina crown. I am here to ensure this happens!"

His eyes swept them with a haughty look, his pale cheeks flushed with his fury, and then he flinched when he spied the tiny girl cowering, peeking around the doorway of the barn.

"Miss Julianna!" he shouted, recovering. "What are you doing here? Be gone! Go back to the House, where you belong!"

He started toward her, waving his arms, towering above her, his face furious at having a witness from the Family of his outrage with the slaves. He moved to grab her, to perhaps carry her bodily away.

This terrified her, and she whirled about, running away from the seeking arms, crying, stumbling, her little yellow skirts flying every which way as she darted between the shacks. Her bare elfin feet pounded the hot dirt paths until she reached a rough shed set under the trees, where she found the solace she sought.

Running inside, "Samma Tahe!" she cried between sobs, "Samma Tahe, Mr. Brown was so mad!" and there he was, sitting at the rough wooden table, shaping a clay base into a small bowl. She fell into his arms, and he lifted her onto his lap.

All was better. Her face was wet from her tears, her short, fair curls were completely tousled, and she was still hiccupping as she started to calm down, but now she was safe.

After a bit, she said, "Samma?"

A rumble came from the chest that supported her back. "Yes, missy?"

"He won't come in here, will he?"

"No, missy Julianna, you know he stays out of Samma's work shed. Clean boots are too important to him," came the soothing reply.

Strong bronze arms surrounded her tiny frame, agile hands winding long snakes of clay around the top of the base, nimble fingers pinching the clay here, expertly smoothing a line there. He dipped his fingers into a cup of water and wet the top edge of the wall, preparing it each time for the next rope of clay. She watched, finger creeping into her mouth, as the pot gradually grew taller, and Samma Tahe started using shells to smooth the cords together.

"Can this one have horses, Samma?" Julianna asked. "I like the ones that have horses."

"It has not spoken yet," said Samma Tahe calmly. "The pot will shape itself, and I must follow where it leads. But I will try to make the spouts into horse heads."

"But don't make them scary mouths, Samma," pleaded Julianna, ducking her head back into Samma Tahe's chest.

He leaned forward a bit, reaching toward the far side of the pot, his silky black hair falling forward like a screen in front of her eyes. On his lap, Julianna could feel the balance in his arms and legs as he worked the clay, his words gently guiding her mind as serenely as his hands molded the clay.

"It is just a pot, missy Julianna. It is made of earth and water and fire," he said. "My people have made these pots for many generations. Sometimes they are just pots, and sometimes they are used for something special."

"Like what?" the tiny girl asked, wiggling her dirty bare toes together.

He put one hand on the curve of the pot, supporting the outer wall as he pushed against the inside with a shell. "We honor our ancestors with our pottery," said Samma Tahe. "We use them to ward off evil spirits. We celebrate the seasons with them."

"But I don't like the scary ones," protested Julianna. She looked at the clay accusingly, as if it were the cause of her recent distress. "They are like Mr. Brown."

"Mr. Brown has a job to do for your Papa," said the calm voice. "Mr. Brown is scared, too."

This was astounding to Julianna.
Mr. Brown, scared?

"He isn't scared!" she said indignantly, sitting up straight, almost hitting Samma Tahe in the chin. "He shouted at me! He shouted at my friends!"

Samma Tahe added more clay to the pot, starting the spouts opposite one another on the upper lip. "Mr. Brown is not sure of his place here yet. He wants to prove his worth to your Papa. He wants the people to obey him, but he does not yet have their respect. This takes time he is not willing to wait," he said.

Julianna reached forward, snagged a scrap of clay, and rolled it into a ball as she thought about this.

He went on, "It is people who cause fear, not objects. In its life this vessel may hold much water or many meals. But it will not create fear.

Only people do. And often the fear is formed in our own minds."

Julianna's brow furrowed. This was hard for a four-year-old to understand.

Samma Tahe went on, his words gentle and measured. "I heard a tale as a young child in my village in the mountains, before I was captured and sold. A grandfather was teaching his grandson about life. He said that inside each of us, there are two wolves. One is evil, and it holds all our anger and jealousy, envy and pride, guilt and greed. The other is good, celebrating joy and kindness, peace and love, hope and truth."

Julianna watched, snuggled in her safe haven, as the spouts began to look like the heads of animals. "Do I have wolves inside me, too?" she asked.

"Oh, yes. All of us do," answered Samma Tahe.

She looked at the clay in her hands, squashing it in the middle with her thumb, separating it into two parts, and then closing her hand around them both, protecting them. "But Samma Tahe, how can the wolves be happy together?" she asked.

"They cannot," he said simply.

She cocked her head. "Then which wolf wins?" she asked.

"That is the very question the grandson asked," answered her guide. "His grandfather had a simple answer: The wolf who wins is the one you feed."

Julianna thought about this. "Feed the wolf?" she questioned, relaxed at last, diverted by the story. She was very comfortable, sheltered in the shade of the shed.

Samma Tahe explained, "If we feed the wolf with fear and anger, it grows bigger and meaner. If we feed it with love and hope, it becomes more peaceful and beautiful. Our outsides show which wolf has won inside."

There was quiet for a bit while Samma Tahe molded the clay delicately. Then, the tiny girl asked sleepily, "Does Mr. Brown feed his wolf wrong?"

"Every person makes their own choice," said Samma Tahe. "It is not my place to judge Mr. Brown." He brought the spouts to a point, opening the mouths wide. "But, missy, which wolf will you feed?" he asked gently.

Julianna's eyes were drowsing. As her eyes opened one more time, she saw that the spouts on the pot were wolves, and they were beautiful. She was not scared of them, for she knew which wolf must be fed and tamed.

She rested her head against Samma Tahe's arm and drifted off, dreaming of running through the mountains, free and light, and a girl with honey-brown hair ran effortlessly beside her.

"Lucie?"

She stirred, letting go of the dream.

"Lucie? You okay, sweetheart?"

She opened her eyes, and her dad's face swam into view. He looked concerned.

"Hi, Dad. Yeah, I'm okay," she said, blinking a little to shake the rest of the dream from her eyes. "I had an ancestor dream."

His expression cleared with relief, and he ran his hand through his light-brown buzz cut.

Sean burst onto the porch steps, disturbing Rotunda who woke with a start in Lucie's lap and laid her little red ears back, shrinking away defensively. "Hey, Dad, where's Lucie? I've got a ton of homework, and with band practice going so late…"

"She's here, Sean," his dad told him. "She says she had an ancestor dream."

"Ancestor dream?" exclaimed Sean. "Hey, Nana!" he called through the screened door. "Lucie had another dream!"

They heard the blender roar, Nana yelp, and then the noise ceased.

"What? Oh, my," was the indistinct reply from inside the house. They could hear her feet hurrying through the hallway, and Nana's bright form emerged onto the porch, wiping pink goo off her face with a purple dish towel.

"I hit the button without the lid on!" she exclaimed. "I hate it when that happens. A dream, Lucie?"

"Was this one unusual?" asked Rob, sitting down in the chair beside Lucie's swing, Nana and Sean drawing close. "I tried to wake you, and you were so deep in that I couldn't."

"I was in dream inside a dream, I think," Lucie explained. "I started in a dream about a little girl called Julianna, and then at the end she fell asleep and dreamed, too. We were running! And I felt so wild and happy and free."

"Good dream, then?" Rob asked.

"Yeesssss," drawled out Lucie. "In the end it was, but she was so scared at the beginning. I want to tell you about it, but first can I call Andrea? We've got a Social Studies extra credit assignment, and we've got to do it on Wednesday!"

"Why Wednesday?" asked Rob.

"Because I have a feeling we've got to go to see pottery, and the only day we can go to the Crack-Stackin' Pottery is Wednesday!"

6

Lucie and Andrea stood, hands on hips, eyebrows furrowed, heads cocked, staring up at a towering pile of clay pots. Stacked on top of each other in a big gully, pots of every size were chunked together in a pyramid, rising to the top of the ravine. In each layer several pots were glazed in bright colors, so an irregular rainbow trickled down. Every pot had a crack in it, and water had been diverted from the nearby creek through a homemade metal sluice system, dumping into the top of the mound. As the water wove its way down the pots, it gushed through the cracks, sounding like wind chimes, with a few whistles letting loose at unusual intervals.

Andrea finally spoke. "I can't decide whether I like it or not."

"I know," Lucie said. "It's got the uggles, but the music is kind of relaxing."

"It reminds me of the inventions in *Chitty Chitty Bang Bang*," said Andrea.

Their moms, Laurel and Serrie, snickered a little.

"I think the tale is, long ago the potters used this gully for pots that were damaged in the kiln during firing," said Laurel, "and eventually the stack got pretty tall. There was a period of intense rain, and the gully became a route for the extra water to reach Kytle Creek. When the water ran through the pots, it made these sounds, and they liked it so much that they built the sluices to have it year-round."

Serrie commented, "It certainly is colorful, and… original!" She had come straight from work in a lovely coral dress that complimented her café-au-lait complexion. Her eyes twinkled as she raised her exquisite dark eyebrows in amusement. "I imagine the business got its name very naturally from this marvel! Let's go see what other surprises the Crack-Stackin' Pottery has in store!"

"Ha, ha, good pun, Mom," teased Andrea as they mounted the steps from the ravine to the parking lot. She elbowed Lucie in the ribs. "Get it, *has in store*?"

"Ouch! Yeah, I get it," said Lucie, rolling her eyes. "They do have a store; I saw it on their website, and a museum, too. Hey, Mom, should we get a picture for Mr. Kishpaugh now, or after we come out?"

"Let's get one now before the sun goes down too much, and the light gets orangey," said Laurel, getting her phone out of her purse.

The two girls stood, arms raised in triumph, under the big **CRACK-STACKIN' POTTERY** sign over the entrance. Laurel and Serrie both snapped pictures with their phones, grinning as the girls struck a few more poses before turning to enter the pottery.

The four of them were greeted in the front room by a plump, dark-skinned woman with an elaborate, entwined hairstyle that wove black, gold and fuchsia braids together, ending in a beautiful up-do. She was dressed casually in a clay-dotted denim shirt and jeans.

"Welcome to the Crack-Stackin' Pottery!" she said with a huge grin. "Laurel, how are you?"

"Oh, I'm great, Zimina, how are you?" Laurel said as she gave her a hug. "You know Serrie Longstreet, don't you?"

"Absolutely! I'm checking out books all the time over at her library," said Zimina, as she and Serrie shook hands.

"We're here on a school project, Zimina," Laurel explained, motioning to the girls. "These are our daughters, Lucie and Andrea, and they have a social studies assignment to visit a local historical site. Can we take the tour?"

"You have come to the right place, and I am at your service!" Zimina chuckled. "Although you could probably give it yourself, Laurel, with as many times as you've been here!

"The Crack-Stackin' Pottery has been in existence for over one hundred years. It was started by Lemuel Possham and his sons, whose pictures you can see here," she said as she motioned to pictures hanging on the walls. "They learned how to throw pots, better known as ware, from a man named Will Hewell from Gillsville in Hall County, who was one of the most respected ware turners of the pottery movement in North Georgia. Lemuel Possham employed traveling potters as well, and the Posshams built their customer base as many did by taking their finished pottery by wagon and later by truck through the mountains to markets.

"It was in the early 1890's that Lemuel's sons Hardy and Sully started making face jugs. One of the traveling potters had taught them the craft, and they soon taught their brothers. Face jugs were a big boost to their income, especially from tourists. They'd even go into Western North Carolina to sell their ware, because wealthy folks liked to spend summers up there, for the cooler weather and the health benefits."

"What about the women in the family?" asked Serrie, stopped at a group picture in front of the pottery. "Weren't they involved?"

"They were very much involved," answered Zimina. "But with the attitudes of the times, they weren't allowed to make their own pots. That was considered men's work until the 1920's when some of Lemuel's granddaughters elbowed their way into the creative side. Their ideas lightened several aspects of the business, from the workload to the colors used in glazes to a more comical look for the face jugs."

"Is this a picture of the pyramid outside?"

asked Andrea, pointing to another framed print.

"You got it. The pottery was originally known as Possham Pottery, but the locals started calling it Crack-Stackin' because of the mound in the gully, and eventually the name stuck.

"But you've come here to see the pottery in action, so I'll stop here and say, *Right This Way!*"

The group followed Zimina through the doorway to a large, open room where various tables, shelves, and equipment were scattered. Zimina took them over to the pottery wheel near the windows. A man in an old KISS tour t-shirt and jeans was throwing a chunk of clay onto the pedestal of the pottery wheel, working it until it was softer. He wiped his brow with the back of his wrist, getting a smear of clay across his forehead and into his short, sandy hair.

"This is Evan," Zimina told them. "He makes the base pots for some of our face jugs."

Evan nodded at them, and then went to work. Lucie watched the spinning clay, the potter's hands shaping it into a round mound, pulling it up, pushing it back down as his feet kicked the wheel base below. She saw him open the top of the mound with his thumbs, gently adding pressure to widen the mouth and pull it taller. Slowly, carefully, Evan pushed the walls between his fingers to expand the pot, adjusting the slope of the outside with a triangular tool, until he eventually created a fat rounded jug, spinning all the while on the wheel. Once the wheel stopped, he took a wire connected to short wooden dowels, held it taut, and sliced the bottom of the pot from the wheel head.

Evan took the pot to a large walk-in closet and carefully set it among other pots on a tall set of shelves.

"It's important, girls, to let the clay dry thoroughly before it's fired," Zimina told them. "If the clay has any moisture in it when it gets into the kiln, it can explode. So, we store the pots that haven't dried completely, called greenware, in here on the shelves. The enclosed space helps the pots dry more evenly. This is also the staging area for our potters to get the pots that will become face jugs."

"Is that how the pots outside got cracks in them?" asked Lucie. "The pots didn't dry enough before they were fired?"

"Some of them, yes," answered Zimina. "Sometimes there is something extra in the clay that we can't see, like a small grasshopper or ant or small stick, that burns off in the firing but leaves an air pocket where the item used to be. That air pocket can make the pot leak or crack."

Continuing the tour, Zimina led the group to a nearby table where another potter was creating a face on a jug. "Miri's specialty is unusual faces," said Zimina.

Miri smiled shyly from under her gray mop of hair, her petite, wrinkled face lighting up as she recognized Laurel. She attached snakes of clay to the top lip of the jug, curving them down on either side to make handles that gave the impression of a little girl's pigtails. Then she took a carrot-shaped piece of clay and attached it to the front of the jug, pressing it in firmly on all sides to get rid of any trapped air.

"I always start with the nose," she said. "It helps me realize the character of the face."

She melded the nose to the jug's clay, using a small sponge to finish removing all traces of connection, and then she pushed her thumbs to either side of the bridge of the nose, making indentations for the eyes. As she added clay, building the eyes, she smoothed the edges with her fingers and the sponge until the slope of the eyelids and then the eyebrows looked completely natural, looking out at the visitors in surprise.

While Laurel and Serrie watched the face emerge from the clay, Andrea pulled Lucie over to the next station, where Zimina was immersing pots in buckets of glaze. Each pot emerged dripping, and then she swirled the glaze, making sure that every inch of the internal walls was covered. She set them on racks, where the excess liquid trickled down the faces to be caught in the pans below.

"That one on the end looks like it's crying!" Andrea whispered to Lucie, a mischievous glint in her eye. "But that one," she said, pointing, "looks like it's sweating after having been at ball practice in ninety-degree heat!"

Lucie giggled.

Grinning at them, Zimina said, "Would you girls like to try it?".

"Sure!" they chorused, and she handed each of them a whimsical coffee mug. Lucie's had a grinning pig's face on it, and Andrea's had a comical man with a handlebar mustache. They dipped the mugs into the glaze, covering them both completely, and then they swirled the glaze on the inside, following Zimina's directions. Emptying the mugs of excess glaze, they carefully deposited their mugs on the rack Zimina indicated.

"Look at you, getting real-time experience!" Laurel exclaimed as she and Serrie joined them.

Zimina laughed, handing each of the girls a towel to wipe their hands, keeping the drips from getting on their t-shirts and shorts. "They're naturals, Laurel, but I shouldn't be surprised, seeing as how Lucie has you as a mother."

"They do muck about in my studio every so often," admitted Laurel. "I send Andrea home more often than not in need of the laundry room!"

Serrie gave her a sour look. "You do not!" she retorted. "Andrea gets that way on her own, running after her little brother and sister!"

"Mom, we need to get more clay for the craft room," said Andrea. "I want to make some of these, and you know the twins love to squish their hands in the clay."

"If you need clay, we can probably accommodate you!" said Zimina with a twinkle. "But first, let's head out of doors."

They moved out into the yard of the pottery, where Zimina explained how the pots were fired. She said that they used a woodburning kiln once a month, and the pots were initially fired at a temperature of 1800 degrees, but then the second firing reached over 2200 degrees Fahrenheit.

"Twenty-two hundred degrees!" Andrea was astounded.

"It has to be that hot for the clay to mature," said Zimina. "And we raise the temperature very slowly over two to eight hours to the first firing, and let it die out gradually after the final firing. It's a delicate process."

She showed them what looked like a rounded hobbit cottage, made of light-colored bricks. It had an open doorway, and she explained to the girls that the kiln was constructed of special firebricks that could withstand the high temperatures. After the pottery was inserted into the kiln, the doorway was bricked up. The temperature itself could be adjusted by removing certain bricks to let air in and heat out.

"You don't have a kiln like this, do you Laurel?" asked Serrie.

"No, mine is electric. It doesn't get the same individual effects that wood burning kilns do, but it's better for controlling bright glazes. I use so many bright colors, it works a little better for many of my creations," said Laurel. "How about the clay, Zimina? Tell the girls where the Posshams got it."

"North Georgia has had a concentration of

potters for over a century partly because of the clay found in this area," said Zimina. "The Posshams, like many other potters, dug their own clay. They were fortunate that they had prime acreage here near Kytle Creek, and a few feet down under the tall grass they hit a great clay bed. They had to mix five different kinds of clay to get the right consistency."

"Was it hard to mix different kinds of clay together?" asked Andrea.

"Oh, yes, they had to grind it. You couldn't use your hands to pull it together," replied Zimina.

"How did they grind it, then?" Lucie asked.

Zimina led them over to a big hole under a shed roof. "They'd put the clay down in here, hitch up a mule on the end of a pole, and lead him round and round, moving paddles to grind the clay, mixing it at the same time. It took hours, but in the end, they'd get what they needed."

"Do you still do that, today?" asked Lucie, wondering where a mule might be kept and if they could go see it.

Zimina laughed. "No, no. We do still dig our own clay for special projects, but we use an electric grinder. Otherwise, we have it shipped in."

"So, where do we get the clay?" asked Andrea, eager to get creative.

Zimina laughed again. "Caught the artistic bug, have you? Come on inside, and I'll *dig* some up for you."

7

Following Zimina, the girls and their mothers trooped back into the pottery, and they all took their time looking around the shelves of the store. As Andrea debated with her mom over the amount of clay to purchase, Lucie wandered into a large connecting room. Here she found more examples of pottery, but they looked much older and had signs and information beside each one. Lucie browsed along, and as she reached the back of the room Zimina joined her.

"Found our museum, have you?" asked Zimina. "Can I answer any questions?"

"Actually, yes," said Lucie hesitantly. "Some of this pottery, the very old-looking ones like these pipes and those statues of people, don't seem to have the same construction as what we saw you making today. Were they made differently?"

"You have a good eye," said Zimina. "These examples were found in Native American archaeological sites. The natives that lived here in McCall County and North Georgia wound ropes of clay on top of one another to build their pots, and then they smoothed the ropes together to meld the walls of the pottery."

"Would the Cherokee have made pots this way?" Lucie asked, thinking of her dream from Monday.

"Certainly, they did, as did the people that were here before the Cherokee, the Mississippians. They moved into this area and displaced the people of the Woodland period. Many of their earthenware was made in this way."

"Were animals important to their culture?" asked Lucie. "I noticed several pots with animals on them."

"Indeed, they were important. This one here," said Zimina as she picked up a decorated bottle, "has birds as its theme, and frequently animal heads were used as decorative spouts for a bottle or jug. One animal important to this area was the wolf."

Lucie's head gave a twitch, and she had a feeling she was getting warmer in her questioning. Andrea bounded in, causing Lucie and Zimina to turn in her direction.

"Hey, Luce! This stuff will be great for our report!" enthused Andrea. "Can I take some pictures, Zimina?"

"Absolutely," Zimina told her.

"I like this one with the wolves on it," remarked Andrea, pulling out her phone and snapping a picture.

"How interesting. I was just mentioning to

Lucie that the wolf was an important animal in the native culture around here," said Zimina.

"My dad has Native American ancestry, and his family claims the wolf as one of their special animals," Andrea explained. She looked at the pictures that adorned the walls. "What are these?" she asked.

"They're pictures of the Kolomoki mounds and the Etowah mounds," said Zimina. "Kolomoki mounds are in South Georgia, and the Etowah mounds are in northwest Georgia. They're excellent examples of towns from a thousand years ago."

"Over here," she went on, motioning to pictures on another wall, "We have pictures of the Nacoochee mound in White County and the Singer-Moye mounds in Stewart County. Archaeologists have been studying and excavating some of these for years, and the state of Georgia protects them."

"Why did the natives make mounds?" wondered Lucie.

"Often they were centers of towns, and a temple would sit atop it or be incorporated into the earthworks," replied Zimina. "A town would frequently be built near running water, to provide access for trade and transportation."

"Their towns couldn't have been too big, could they?" said Andrea. "Their building materials weren't as permanent as ours."

"Some towns and mounds were quite large.

The Singer-Moye site has eight mounds, and the Etowah site is fifty-four acres with the mounds around two rectangular plazas. The largest mound at Kolomoki is fifty-seven feet high, and there were eleven mounds there," replied Zimina.

"Wow! And the archaeologists found this pottery or some like it in the mounds as they excavated?" asked Andrea.

"Oh, yes," said Zimina. "Archaeologists often find caches of ceramic pottery in these sites, depicting animals or people. A person's cup, plate, or pipe was personal to them, and often special items were buried with them. A very important person, a chief or town leader, might be buried in the temple, and their valuables would be symbols to take with them on the next journey."

"Would arrowheads be considered valuable symbols?" asked Andrea.

Zimina shook her head. "I wouldn't think so necessarily, but you'd never know what someone would value. Why do you ask?"

"We were at Shuford Lodge last weekend, and we noticed an arrowhead embedded in the basement floor," said Lucie. "It caught our attention."

Andrea snorted. "Boy, did it!" She cut her eyes at Lucie. "So did that room of face jugs."

"Shuford Lodge?" Zimina's face grew still and watchful. "A room of face jugs?"

"Yeah, we were helping with the Festival," said Lucie. "Mr. Roderick said the jugs were in storage for an upcoming exhibit. There was a lot of lightning, and a power outage, and they took me by surprise."

"Speaking of the Festival," said Andrea, changing direction, "there were so many booths that had things I wanted to buy! And I'm glad I saved some of my money! My mom said I could get something here. I saw lots of small animal sculptures in your gift shop, like chickens and pigs—they were so cute! But I didn't see any wolves. I could get a present for my dad if you had one."

"No, we don't do any wolves here," said Zimina rather stiffly, and Lucie got the impression that she was very done with the conversation.

"Why not?" asked Andrea, puzzled.

"Just personal preference," Zimina said lightly, but she started moving toward the door as she spoke. "Did you find the clay you wanted, Andrea?"

"Yeessssss," drew out Andrea, and she stared as Zimina disappeared into the shop.

Andrea turned to look at Lucie. "What just happened?" she asked.

Lucie was as befuddled as Andrea. "I dunno," she replied. "She couldn't stop talking about the native mounds, and then we mention the Shuford Lodge…"

"And face jugs, which they make here," put in Andrea, "and then wolves, after she'd brought it up to start with…"

"And then she totally closed up!" finished Lucie.

They started toward the door of the museum, and they heard Zimina talking to their mothers, back to her jolly self. "You betcha! Honeydew Farms makes the best jams and jellies! That's why we keep a little corner here for them. You'd never know it, but Carmen Littlegalle is a distant cousin of mine!"

Andrea grabbed Lucie's arm. "Wasn't that the Honeydew Farms booth where we saw the *wet hen* lady on Saturday?" she said in a low voice.

"Yeah!" whispered Lucie excitedly. "And Sean asked Mom what her name was, and she said Carmen Littlegalle! What a coincidence!"

"A coincidence? I think not!" said Andrea decidedly. "We've got a hot clue, and the ancestors are poking us!"

"But what does it mean?" wondered Lucie.

The girls stared at each other.

Andrea's mom Serrie suddenly appeared in the doorway, startling them.

"Ahhh!" said Andrea, jumping.

"Are you okay?" Serrie asked, concerned.

"Oh, yeah. This mystery just keeps getting weirder and weirder," said Andrea, shaking her head.

"Really? You'll have to fill me in. Are you two ready to go?" asked Serrie. "Laurel's already gone to the car."

They started walking toward the door. Then something prompted Andrea to say, "Mom, could Grandma Rose come to Lucie's quilting party this Saturday?" Then she blinked and looked surprised.

Serrie said, "I'm sure they would welcome her, Andrea, but you just saw Grandma last weekend."

"Okay. I guess you're right," said Andrea, and she followed her mom and Lucie out of the store. As she stepped through the doorway, she tripped and hurtled forward into their bodies.

"Ooof!" she cried, and they crashed to the wooden porch floor.

"Yeah, Mom, we gotta call Grandma Rose," said Andrea in a muffled voice. Lucie groaned as she tried to move from under Andrea.

"What's happened?" cried Zimina from inside. She hurried to them. "Oh, I should have warned you. I trip over that all the time. We've tried to fix that spot in the doorway, but the planks always move back." She helped them up.

"No worries, Zimina," said Serrie, picking up her shopping and peeking in the bag to make sure nothing was broken.

Laurel brought the minivan around, and they piled in, waving to Zimina and calling their thanks. Then as they pulled out of the driveway, Andrea said, "Mom, can we call Grandma Rose NOW?" and Lucie nodded her agreement vigorously.

8

It was Friday night, and Lucie was home with her mom. Sean, being a member of the McCall County High School marching band, was traveling to Habersham Central High School to perform at the football game, and their dad was there, too, in his role as Prop Crew Band Dad. They had come back to the house twice before they made it to the school for departure, however, since Sean had first forgotten his band hat and then, half a mile down the road, remembered he'd left his trumpet in the kitchen.

Lucie was sitting up in bed, dressed in her favorite purple pajama set, propped up on big fluffy pillows. She was sparking with creativity. She had stickers, tape, fine markers, ribbon, glue, glitter, and scissors at hand, and spread out on her lapboard was the zine she was making. She'd seen a video online for making zines, mini magazines from folded paper to give to friends, and her first attempt was going well. She'd found images of black and white flowers, rainbows, and cartoon characters online, and she'd printed them out. Now she was arranging and coloring them, using all sorts of pretties to accent them, including quotes she particularly liked.

It had been a long week, and tomorrow was going to be full, too, first with the quilting bee at Nana and Pop's, then a band competition for Sean later in the day. But she was fired up, and her eyes flashed, her mind zipping from one idea to another, grabbing the next color, cutting out the next image.

Her mom stuck her head in the door, Carson appearing a split second later at her feet. He charged into the room and threw his front feet up on Lucie's bed, rear-end wagging and tongue lolling, his eyes hopeful of a lift.

Laurel laughed and came on into the room. "He is absolutely spoiled!" she said, lifting Carson's short hind legs and giving him a boost onto Lucie's bed. He turned around, laughing at Laurel, and then found his fleece blanket, turned around three times, and *floomped* down upon it, his long ears flying up on his way down.

Her mom sat on a spot of the bed not covered with paper or supplies. "Your zine looks amazing!" she said. "Who are you giving it to?"

"I think I'll scan it on Dad's scanner and then print out several on the color printer. I want Andrea to have one, and Emily. I bet Amy would like the idea, too. She's so precise, I bet hers would look as polished as the ones in the video," said Lucie. "Gran might even like one."

"I love your creation," her mom said

admiringly. "You know it's getting late, though? You ought to turn in, with such a big day tomorrow. You ready for it?" she asked.

"Oh, yeah!" Lucie beamed. "I can't wait! I know I can't have my quilt until my birthday after Christmas, but it will be so exciting to see it spread out!"

"I love the fabrics you chose," said Laurel. "They are so like you, and the quilt will look great here in your room."

Lucie yawned. "I hope so."

Laurel laughed. "See, the power of suggestion and you're already yawning. Need some help moving your supplies?"

Lucie considered, then nodded. "Thanks, Mom."

They stacked Lucie's supplies on the lap board, and then Laurel carefully transferred the load over to Lucie's desk. Lucie dumped a few pillows off the bed, then scooted down under her covers. It was snuggly, as the weather had finally turned, and there was a crisp to the air. It made her think of pumpkins and apple cider.

Laurel leaned over, gave her a kiss on the forehead, and reached to turn off the bedside light. "Goodnight, sweetheart," she said, and turned to leave.

"Goodnight, Mom," said Lucie sleepily, and she pulled the covers closer over her shoulders. She lay gazing at the stars through her skylight for a while, thinking about what she wanted to put on her zine next, but eventually she relaxed and was pulled firmly and inexorably into a deep sleep.

Wiltwyck
(Later known as Kingston, New York)
September 1667

He was running. His bare feet pounded the earth, carrying him through the towering, dense forest.

"I'll get you, Pieter!" he shouted joyfully, as he spied movement up ahead.

An answering giggle floated back to him, and he spurred himself faster along the path, underbrush whipping against the breeches covering his legs as he made the curve, his brown hair streaming straight back from the wind in his face. He saw a flash of movement out of the corner of his eye, and he turned his head just in time to see buckskin leggings disappearing behind a tree. He stopped, stock-still in the middle of the path.

"Nanichi?" he called.

The leggings came into sight again, along with a bare chest, bare feet, and shoulder-length black hair. "Johannes? Yoon ndápi!"

"Nanichi! Pieter, come here! Nanichi is here!" he cried and ran forward.

Nanichi ran towards him, and the two boys met, giggling and chasing each other around trees. Pieter reappeared quickly, and the three boys played and wrestled until they flopped onto the moss of the forest floor, panting. Johannes's white shirt was smudged from the horseplay.

Nanichi was the first to sit up. He looked at the two boys solemnly. "Nkata kèku lël," he said.

"What did he say, Johannes?" asked Pieter.

"He said he wants to tell us something," said Johannes, sitting up and tucking his legs underneath him.

"May lël. Lël kwënakwsu òk màxkalhùkwe," said Nanichi.

"He wants us to tell Captain Chambers something," said Johannes.

"How do you know?" asked Pieter.

"*Lël* is 'tell'. And he wants us to tell the tall man*, kwënakwsu*, with red hair, *màxkalhùkwe*," said Johannes. "Who else could that be?" He looked at Nanichi. "*Ntëla. Kèku hèch?* I tell him. What? What is it?" He held his hands out, palms up.

Nanichi took a stick, pushed aside some leaves, and drew in the earth. Pieter and Johannes moved over beside him and watched as Nanichi's picture took shape, becoming mountains with a squiggly line at the bottom, a group of people below it.

"Máchu-awéen. Síipoong wŭneewáawal, òhchuwike," said Nanichi.

"He saw a bad man at the river, among the mountains," said Johannes.

"Didn't some of the new English soldiers take Captain Chambers to scout for land grants near a river last week?" asked Pieter, scratching his blond curls.

Nanichi pointed to one of the stick figures that was head and shoulders above the others. "Kwënakwsu òk màxkalhùkwe," and then drew a circle around some of the others. "Máchu-awéen."

"Captain Chambers was with bad men?" Johannes wondered. "Why are they bad?"

"Ask him!" urged Pieter.

"Nanichi, *kòch*... what is the word for bad?" Johannes asked Pieter.

"Ummm... Try *mahchikwi*," answered Pieter.

"Nanichi, *kòch mahckiwi*? Why bad?" asked Johannes, tapping on the circle of men in the dirt.

"Máchu-awéen kahta mpatamweikaonëna," replied Nanichi.

"*Kahta*... They want," said Johannes to Pieter. "Bad men want... but that last word... what was it?"

Pieter shrugged. Johannes asked Nanichi, "*Chich*? Again?"

"Máchu-awéen kahta mpatamweikaonëna," repeated Nanichi.

"*Mpatamweikaonëna*," said Johannes slowly.

"Ahikta!" nodded Nanichi in approval. "Mpatamweikaonëna! Ehòlënt."

Johannes frowned. "I don't know that one, either."

Nanichi stood up. "Mëxumsa, sakima, ntalukalùkw. Làpich knewël." He began to walk away.

"*Làpich knewël*, Nanichi," called Johannes.

"Wait, he's going?" Pieter cried, jumping to his feet. "What did he say?"

"His grandfather, *mëxumsa,* the chief or *sakima*, sent him to talk to us," explained Johannes, rising as well. "Then we said goodbye."

Nanichi was just visible through the trees. "Just like that? We were playing!" grumped Pieter, hands on hips, watching him go.

"You know they disappear quickly," said Johannes. "I think we'd better go find my father, and Captain Chambers. If the chief sent him…"

"It's a good thing Captain Chambers has been working with you and your brothers on translating," said Pieter. "I'd be good at it, too, if I went to see him more."

The boys started to run again, nipping out of the woods back onto the path, running as fast as they could to beat the other. Pieter, short and lithe, pulled far ahead again, and before long they reached the fields that their families shared. Johannes burst out of the forest, gasping for breath, and he was tackled from the side by Pieter who was lying in wait. The two boys hurtled to the ground, rolling down the slope and thudding to a stop at the edge of the field.

They lay there for a moment, laughing, then they clambered to their feet.

"Johannes!" came the call across the field.

"PaPa?" he answered.

"Be careful of the squash. It has just come ripe."

"Yes, PaPa," he answered, and looked at his friend, frowning. "You heard him, Pieter. Be careful of the squash."

"I will be careful of the squash," Pieter mimicked solemnly, and then the two boys dissolved into laughter again.

They hurriedly picked their way across the huge field that several families shared, through the squash and then the corn and the beans, and they reached Johannes's father, who was weeding one of the rows.

"PaPa, we just saw Nanichi in the woods!" said Johannes excitedly. "He was sent by his grandfather, the *sakima*, to deliver a message. We need to see Captain Chambers!"

"He is at Foxhall this morn," said his father. He stood up and brushed his dirty hands off on his homespun trousers. "A message for Thomas, eh? Perhaps we can catch him before he gets too far into his chores."

He headed off at a brisk pace, the boys close on his heels. They took the path to Foxhall, Thomas Chambers's home, and although the day was young the sun cut through the changing leaves at a sharp angle, blinding them at odd moments. The oak, hickory, and chestnut trees were huge, having grown for hundreds of years undisturbed, and small animals rustled in the underbrush and in the trees. Johannes hoped they would not meet a skunk this time.

"How are your parents, Pieter?" asked Johannes's father. "I have not seen them in some days."

"They are well, Mr. Westvaal. Thank you for asking," replied Pieter somewhat formally. Then he returned to his usual mischievous self, speaking to Johannes.

"This is the spot in the path where you usually tell me you were born at Foxhall, eight years ago," teased Pieter. "Do you not want to tell me again?"

Johannes moved to push him, but Pieter danced out of the way. "Well, I was born there. It is the greatest house of our settlement!"

"Where we are born and where we die are not for us to decide," said his father. "You were born, that should be enough."

They came out of the woods into a clearing, and in the center of it was a large square house with a pyramid of a roof. It had windows trimmed with shutters on each side as well as in the roof, and a tall chimney rose up the front of the house to the right of the center front door. The well was to the left of the house, and chickens scurried away from them as they approached.

"Hello, Foxhall!" called Johannes's father.

"What, Jurian Westvaal?" was the response, and from behind the house toward the stables a tall, redheaded man appeared. His welcoming smile was echoed in his energetic stride, and he reached the small party with arms wide. "What brings you here this day? And with such able assistants!" he said with a grin for the small boys.

"Johannes and Pieter have a tale to tell, Thomas," said Jurian.

Johannes quickly told Captain Chambers about their time with Nanichi, with Pieter interjecting when he felt Johannes wasn't being thorough enough. Captain Chambers was concerned.

"I was with bad men?" he wondered. "But the Munsees and the other tribes have been much happier since the Dutch turned the colony over to the English, and our dealings with them have been much more peaceful. What is more, the soldiers with me were English." He thought a minute. "Tell me again the last bit he said."

"He said, *Mpatamweikaonëna! Ehòlënt*," Johannes told him.

"Ehòlënt is the word for beloved," said Thomas Chambers. "But the other is unfamiliar."

"We have tried to be fair with the Munsees," said Jurian. "But even you, who translates and mediates disputes for our colony, have had misunderstandings over land. Is it possible we are heading into another sticky situation without realizing it?"

"Of course it is possible," said Thomas Chambers. "We were down by the river, in the mountains. The English were looking at some hills they wanted to clear and build upon. Small ones, and I could not understand why they were attractive to them."

"I have been asked to guide another English scouting group in the coming weeks," said Jurian. "They said they needed someone familiar with the area. I will keep my eyes open for trouble."

Johannes felt uneasy. "PaPa, Nanichi said the soldiers wanted something beloved to the Munsees. Is it safe to go out with the soldiers?"

Jurian put a calming hand on his son's shoulder. "I have lived forty-seven years, my son, and thirty-four of those years were in this new country. I know the ways of the Munsees, and I will respect them. I will ask the soldiers to do the same." He squeezed Johannes's shoulder comfortingly.

"But, PaPa," protested Johannes. "You know what Captain Chambers said about the Munsee name. It means *wolf,* and..."

"And you must be cautious of wolves, for they are not tame, nor should be," finished Thomas Chambers. He and Jurian exchanged a look.

Jurian crouched down beside his son. "Johannes, let me ask you something," he said. "When you were with Nanichi today, were you scared?"

Johannes looked at his father in astonishment. "No! Nanichi is my friend!"

"But you are Dutch. And he is Munsee," said Jurian. "He is of the wolf people."

Johannes shook his head. "Nanichi would never hurt us. We played together!"

Thomas Chambers said, "The wolf is a strong and proud being, and the Munsees are well named."

He paused, then said, "We may not know which way the wolf will turn, but we must keep believing in the possibilities of peace. You boys and Nanichi have the right way of it."

"Keep that friendship, Johannes," said Jurian, squeezing Johannes's shoulder. "Keep talking and playing, too. Captain Chambers and I will do our part as well, to further harmony with the grown Munsees and the other tribes in this land."

He stood up. "We will see you soon, Thomas! But the weeds are calling. Come, boys, or Pieter's parents will be searching for him!"

He clasped Thomas's hand briefly in his and then started toward the path to the fields the families shared for safety. The boys ran ahead, abandoning the seriousness of the conversation in a race that was as natural as breathing to the young.

Lucie surfaced from sleep, vaguely aware in the deep dark of her brother entering his room next door. He made a few soft noises, getting ready for bed after a late band-bus ride home. Reassured, sleep gently carried Lucie away once more.

9

Lucie set the veggie platter down carefully on the picnic table and then took stock of the offerings. They had laid out the lunch outside Gran's carriage house, well covered in plastic wrap and weighted down in case a breeze got too strong, and Pop had set up card tables nearby with folding chairs. Lucie could hear chatter through the open doors of Gran's house where two quilting frames had been erected, women plying their needles through the thick fabric layers almost as fast as their tongues wagged. Lucie's birthday ancestor quilt, a tradition in her family for a girl's thirteenth birthday, was on one frame, its blocks of pink and yellow fabric cheery splashes of color. Stretched across the other frame was a Basket Weave quilt in warm autumn hues. It was going to be auctioned off soon by the local Quilters Circle to raise funds for charity.

"I've got the paper plates," said Andrea, coming up behind her. "That's the last of what was in the kitchen. You think we can have a break?"

"I think so," said Lucie. "They ought to stop pretty soon for lunch. You hungry?"

"Not yet," said Andrea. "I really want to know more about your dream from last night."

"Let's go up in Gran's loft," suggested Lucie. "Sean's up there hiding out, and he knows more about Gran's genealogy program than I do."

The girls went in Gran's carriage house, which had been refinished and refurbished to her precise specifications when she came to live on Pop and Nana's property after her husband had died. The lower floor was an open room, complete with small kitchen, living room, and bedroom all in one. She'd paneled the room in light honey oak, and the quilts and pictures she'd hung completed her little nest. Her small bathroom jutted out into the room a little, snuggling up into the stairwell that led upstairs to the loft. At ninety-two years old, she had everything she wanted: privacy, convenience, and family close by at the "big house."

Today, however, her antique four-poster bed had been dismantled and her furniture pushed back against the walls or removed from the room. Gran was in her element, stationed at one of the quilting frames, listening to the chatter around her and putting in her own two-cents-worth more often than not. She looked up as the girls entered the room and touched the hand of the woman next to her and nodded in the direction of the girls. The woman, Andrea's grandma, looked up from her sewing and twinkled her eyes at them as they made a fast escape up the staircase.

"Isn't there some machine that can quilt those layers together?" asked Andrea as they passed picture after picture lining the stairwell walls.

"Yeah, Nana sometimes takes hers over to a quilting shop in Hartwell, but they wanted to have a party," said Lucie. "The Historical Society and the Quilters Circle love a chance to get together!"

They emerged at the top of the stairs in Gran's loft. Like the stairwell, the walls were packed with framed family pictures, lit with golden October light from the wonderful windows. Sean sat at the far end of the big library table that dominated the center of the room, his computer open and books surrounding him.

"Hey, Sean, you got a minute?" asked Lucie. "Andrea and I want to research my dream from last night."

Sean didn't seem to hear her. "Look, he's got his earbuds in," said Andrea. She scooted down the length of the table and waved her hand in front of Sean. "Hey, Sean!"

Sean looked up, surprised, and then pulled his earbuds out of his ears. "Hey, guys. What's up?" he asked.

"Lucie and I want to research her dream from last night," said Andrea. "Can you help us?"

Sean stretched. "Sure. But isn't it almost time for lunch?"

"Lunch is set up on the picnic tables outside," said Lucie, "but the quilters get first dibs.

We thought we'd come up here where it's a little safer."

"Pick a little, talk a little?" quoted Sean.

"Huh?" Andrea was puzzled.

"Mom loves *The Music Man*," said Sean. "There's a whole song sung by this group of women, chattering about another one, and they're like hens pecking at insects. That gabble downstairs reminded me of it."

He looked at Lucie. "So why can't you look things up yourself?"

Lucie said, holding up her hands, "I can, but you're better at Gran's genealogy program, and anyway, I pricked my fingers a few times downstairs when I was helping with my quilt. I'm not great at sewing to begin with, but Nana said I needed to be a part of the quilting. My fingers hurt."

Sean stood, walked around the table, and then sat down in front of a laptop. He opened it, entered the password, and then made a few clicks with the mouse.

"Okay, I've got her program pulled up. What names are we looking for?" he asked. Lucie scooted down the table to sit beside him, and Andrea slid in to the seat on his other side.

"They said Westvaal. I don't know how to spell it exactly... and the dad was Jurian and the son was Johannes," Lucie told him.

"*Westvaal*," Sean said quietly, tapping the keys. "It became Westfall later, but... Here's Jurian

Juriansen Westvaal, married to Marretje Hansen, and they were the parents of six kids, one of whom was Johannes Jurian Westvaal. Looks like Jurian and Marretje were born in the Netherlands, and Jurian came to live in New Amsterdam in 1642, when he was thirteen years old, all by himself."

"Where is New Amsterdam?" asked Andrea.

"It's what is known as New York City today," said Sean. "It started as a Dutch settlement."

"That makes sense!" said Lucie. "They talked about being Dutch, and Jurian said he'd been in this country a certain number of years. Why would he come by himself, as a teenager?" she wondered.

"This doesn't say, but he was an indentured servant, or maybe an apprentice, until he was twenty-one years old," explained Sean. "The notes here say he was under the patronship of two men, one of them a wealthy diamond merchant. But he got a patent for land in 1654, in some place called Esopus."

Andrea started tapping on her phone. "I've got my maps app… Esopus is in New York State, about two hours from New York City."

Lucie went back to the computer screen. "Can you click on Johannes?" she asked.

Sean did so, and then said, "Looks like the families moved away from the city for some reason. He was born in what is now Kingston, New York, at a place called Foxhall."

"He said he was!" exclaimed Lucie. "He was really proud of it, and his friend Pieter was teasing him about it. The Captain they went to see, Thomas Chambers, lived there."

Andrea moved the map around on her phone with her finger. "Look! Kingston is right here near Esopus."

Sean checked in the notes section of the file on Johannes. "Says here, Johannes's family had a close relationship with Thomas Chambers, who was tall, red-headed, energetic, and a leader in the community. And that Johannes married a girl who lived across the street from his stepfather."

"Wait, stepfather?" asked Andrea. "Jurian was his stepfather?"

"No," said Sean. "Johannes was Jurian's son. His stepfather was a guy named Jacob Jansen."

"But that means Jurian wasn't around! Did Jurian die?" asked Lucie.

Sean backtracked through the program. "He died in 1667, when Johannes was eight years old. Jurian was guiding a scouting party of English soldiers, not long after they took over the colony from the Dutch, and although the Dutch and the natives had gotten along well with each other recently, some natives shot arrows at the group. Jurian was hit, and he died."

Lucie looked stricken. "Oh, no!! But that's just what he said! He was going to lead a group of soldiers to look for land grants, and Johannes was really upset, because Nanichi had warned the boys about 'bad men' wanting something beloved. He didn't want his father to go."

"What's that about something beloved?" a voice asked from the stairwell. Their heads turned to see the round, friendly face of Andrea's Grandma Rose emerge slowly, and the rest of her followed, carrying a plate of food and a drink with her.

"Grandma Rose!" said Andrea. "Is it time for lunch?"

"Indeedy it is," her Grandma replied. "I thought I'd come to see what's doin' up here. Hi, Sean. I didn't get to say hello downstairs."

"Hi, Mrs. Longstreet," replied Sean. "You've been pulled into the mystery, too?"

"Oh, yes, what fun this is," she said, depositing her lunch on the table. Settling her well-cushioned frame heavily into a chair she said, "Why don't the three of you go grab some of that bountiful spread downstairs, then hop back here, and we can have a good gab?"

Sean, Andrea, and Lucie needed no further urging. Since most of the guests had served themselves and were seated, chatting away, they made quick work of putting together their plates. In nothing flat, they were back upstairs, digging in.

"So, Lucie, tell me about what's going on with you," said Grandma Rose, munching on a cheese-laden stick of celery. "Andrea's told me a bit about your dreams, and the wondrous mysteries you've been solving."

"It's really exciting. This new mystery seems to have something to do with wolves and Native Americans, because they have been in two of my dreams. The first dream didn't have them, but it seemed to say that a message had finally gotten to the right person, and just in time, too, because you never know what's around the bend in the road. The next dream had a native man in it, and he was a potter. I'm not sure he was a slave, but he had been at some point, and the little girl, Julianna, went to him when she was upset. He comforted her and told her a story about everyone having two wolves inside them," explained Lucie.

"I know that story," said Grandma Rose. "It's an old Cherokee teaching tale." She took a bite of pasta salad. "What about the third dream?"

"Last night's dream was really different," said Lucie. "It's the first dream I've had from a boy. His name was Johannes, and he was playing in the forest with his friends Pieter and Nanichi. Nanichi was a native boy, and he had come to send a warning to the settlers. He spoke in his own language, but Johannes had learned some of his language and could translate a lot of it."

"Was he Cherokee?" asked Grandma Rose.

Lucie shook her head. "No. He was Munsee, and from our research it looks like they were living in what is now New York State, in the mid-1600's." She picked up her sandwich and started in on it.

"Munsee," mused Grandma Rose. "I don't know anything about them." She thought a minute, then asked, "I understand why you've picked up on wolves for the dream with the Cherokee potter, but why do you think the dream last night is about wolves?"

Lucie swallowed her bite. "When the boys went to tell the adults about the message Nanichi brought, there was discussion about the fact that the name *Munsee* means *wolf*."

"Ah," said Grandma Rose. "That makes sense. Interesting. Our word, the Cherokee word, for wolf is very different. It is 'waya.' But what is this about a message?"

Sean pushed back his chair. "Excuse me a minute. I'm going down for seconds. Does anyone want dessert?" he asked.

"Can you get me a chocolate chip cookie?" asked Lucie.

"I want a brownie—no, two!" said Andrea. "Those ones with the caramel in the middle."

"Okay," said Sean. "Anything for you, Mrs. Longstreet?"

"No, thank you, Sean, I think I have enough here for now," replied Grandma Rose, eyes twinkling at him.

"Sure thing," he said, disappearing down the stairs.

Lucie went on, "Nanichi was sent to warn Captain Chambers, one of the leaders of the Dutch settlement. He said that the English soldiers who had been exploring with Captain Chambers wanted something beloved to the Munsees, but that they should stay away from it. He also used another word that none of them knew to describe this beloved place. Even Captain Chambers didn't know it."

Andrea pushed her empty plate away from her. "Grandma, what would Native Americans consider beloved?"

"I can't speak for the Munsees specifically," said Grandma Rose, "but I'd think graves would be considered beloved or sacred, a place to worship would be, some place old that had traditions surrounding it would be as well. A gathering place, perhaps, that had been used for many generations for ceremonies, might qualify. In the 1600's this land was still very much as it had been for hundreds, even thousands of years. It certainly was very unchanged when the Cherokee came to this area."

"Haven't the Cherokee always lived in these mountains, Grandma?" asked Andrea.

"Oh, no, dear. Our people, the Cherokees, came into the Appalachians from the north and displaced the Mississippian people between, oh, 1200 and 1600 I think, and the Mississippians had taken over from the Woodland people before that. They may have lived in some of the same places, used some of them for rituals, honored special achievements, absorbed some of the people themselves into their culture," said Grandma Rose.

Sean reappeared, his plate piled high again with food. Andrea snorted.

"What?" Sean protested. "I've got a marching competition tonight. I've got to stock up!"

He handed Lucie a chocolate chip cookie on a napkin and turned to Andrea. "Two caramel brownies, my lady!" he said, handing them to her with a flourish. She giggled, and she took them, carefully cradling them on their festive fall napkin and starting to nibble on one immediately.

"Grandma," she started, then had to get another delectable bite. "Didn't the Cherokee create a written language?"

Grandma Rose nodded. "Yes. The creator was a man named Sequoyah. Look it up on your phone."

Andrea pulled her phone out of her pocket again and started tapping. "Here it is. It says he created symbols for syllables, between 1809 and 1821. And they had a newspaper!"

"What's the symbol for wolf?" wondered Lucie.

"Here's a chart." Andrea got up and stood between her grandma and Lucie. "But I can't make sense of it."

Her grandma chuckled. "You'd have to know how it all works. But you see this symbol that looks like a fancy G?" She pointed at the phone.

"Yeah?" said Andrea.

"Here, Sean, can I borrow a piece of paper?" asked Grandma Rose, pulling a pen out of her pocket.

"No problem," Sean said as he opened one of his binders and took out a piece of loose-leaf paper, scooting it down the table to the girls.

Lucie handed it to Grandma Rose, who drew an upper-case G with an extra flourish at the end, then beside it, a figure that almost looked like a dog's smiling face, with a fancy nose or mustache, with no eyes.

"Waya," said Grandma Rose. "It has a hint of an h with the W, so it sounds like *whae-ya*."

"What about *thank you*?" asked Lucie with a smile.

"Thank you is *wado*," replied Grandma Rose. She drew its symbol on the paper as well. It was very like waya, starting with the fancy upper-case G, but the second symbol looked like an upper-case V.

"Then, *wado*, Mrs. Longstreet!" Lucie said. "I really appreciate your talking with us today."

"Oh, Lucie, I've enjoyed it!" said Grandma Rose, rising from her chair. "I don't get down this way as much as I'd like. I got to see Andrea and Serrie, and I heard a bit of news about my cousin Betty's kids earlier this morning that got me all excited. So, it's been a lovely time."

"Cousin Betty?" said Andrea. "I don't know any Cousin Betty."

"Andrea, girl, you have more cousins in these mountains than you know. They're everywhere! Shake a stick, and you'll find one! Betty and I go way back," chuckled Grandma Rose.

Grandma Rose put an arm around both girls and hugged the two of them at the same time. "You're good girls," she said, and released them.

She picked up her emptied dinnerware and turned to go. "I'd better get back to the quilts! I might miss some more news! But," she said thoughtfully, "I may have to see if there's any of that chocolate pie Sean's eating left for the taking."

Sean surfaced from his pie and gave her a thumbs up. "It's Nana's recipe, so it's excellent!"

"I'll go see! Donadagohvi!" she called to them as she slowly lowered her short bulk down the stairs.

"What does that mean?" Lucie wondered.

"Donadagohvi means, *'Til we meet again!*" Andrea said with a grin.

"Kind of like *au revoir*," commented Sean.

"With all the languages we're getting into, we may need to carry a translator around with us," said Lucie, picking up the remnants of her lunch.

"Or the Tardis from *Doctor Who*!" suggested Andrea.

"I'd rather have the communicator badge from *Star Trek*," said Sean, packing up his computer. "It's a lot smaller than the Tardis."

"Except for that episode where it starts shrinking with the Doctor inside it," Andrea reminded him.

"Lucie! Andrea!" Nana's voice called up the stairs.

"Here!" called Lucie.

"Come on down! We're starting the quilts again!" Nana called. "Sean! Your dad wants to leave soon. You've got that run-through of the show before the buses leave for the marching competition."

"Coming!" Sean responded, dumping his books and binders into his backpack, grabbing his computer bag, and beating a fast exit behind the two girls down the stairs.

10

"Good afternoon, everyone," said Mr. Kishpaugh in his deep voice from the back of the social studies room. "Happy Tuesday! We are about to embark on a journey through time, so I need your full and undivided attention."

He paused and waited for Tommy and Tristan to stop talking. "We've been exploring McCall County and its residents from the past two hundred years. Many of your families were among the first settlers of McCall, and the stories you have shared about them have been fascinating. Now we're going to dig in a different way."

With a few clicks on the touchpad of his computer, he brought up the school homework portal. "Please look at the screen. I've created a PDF of McCall County maps, and they are taken from different points in time. Here is a split screen of four of the maps. Do you see any similarities or differences?"

Tommy's hand shot up. "They're all rectangular?" The room groaned.

Amy gave Tommy a withering look and raised her hand. "Most of them have the major towns marked, but the towns aren't the same size in each, and the topography is depicted differently."

Mr. Kishpaugh nodded approvingly. "Thank you, Amy. Just as a review, what is the meaning of the word topography?" He looked around. "Cynthia?"

Cynthia Jones was winding her hair around her finger and looked a little unsure. "Ummm, isn't it the mountains and rivers and stuff?"

"Yes, all the natural and artificial features of the area," confirmed Mr. Kishpaugh. "What might have influenced the map maker to represent the topography differently?"

Tristan raised his hand. "How about the year the map was created?"

"Why would that affect it?" asked Mr. Kishpaugh, settling his large frame onto a stool.

"Older maps would have less confirmed information," said Tristan. "The mapmakers would have relied on visuals collected on foot, and very old maps might have been made by explorers who were traveling and only recorded what was on their route."

"But what about surveyors?" asked Amy. "George Washington was a surveyor in the mid-1700s. They had that technology, at least."

"Good points, both of you," said Mr. Kishpaugh. "As you proceed through the assignment, keep an open mind, make comparisons, and be a detective. Not all is what it seems, and not all is what it was."

"We ought to ace this, then," whispered Andrea to Lucie. Lucie grinned back at her.

"What else do you see?" asked Mr. Kishpaugh.

Tristan piped up again. "They seem to be written in different languages."

"Why do you say that?" Mr. Kishpaugh asked.

"Two of them are hard to read. The writing style has a lot of flourishes. And the words aren't in English," responded Tristan.

"They've got abbreviations, too," Tommy said.

"There aren't any abbreviations," objected Cynthia.

"Yeah, there are. Look on the top left one," said Tommy.

Mr. Kishpaugh double clicked on the map Tommy indicated, and it pulled up full size.

"Where, Tommy?" he asked.

"Upper left corner, in the mountains, with the river running around it. See, there's a G and then something else," pointed Tommy. Mr. Kishpaugh zoomed in on the area. "See, it almost looks like a cartoon face, but it doesn't have any eyes."

"Wait…" Andrea said slowly. She and Lucie exchanged a long look, then Andrea said, "Mr.

Kishpaugh, my grandma is part Cherokee. She was here last weekend, and we were talking about the Cherokee language and the symbols that were used when it was created."

"You think these are Cherokee symbols?" asked Amy.

"I do. I think they're the symbols for wolf," said Andrea.

"Wolf? Why would someone name a place *wolf*?" scoffed Amy, tossing her blonde head.

"I live on Wolf Place," piped up Karen Sullins.

"And I live in Forests of Wolf subdivision," put in Jamil Tars.

"Ok, ok, I give," said Amy, holding up her hands in surrender.

Mr. Kishpaugh said, "You're already making some astute observations. So, continue that! Your assignment is to work in teams of two, creating a McCall County map of your own, drawing from historical as well as current information. Make sure you include locations that you mentioned or visited for your project last week. Then, use the online map app and create a tour of these locations. They may not be in existence anymore if they come from the historical maps, but you should come as close as you can to where they would be in present day."

"Mr. Kishpaugh, what do we use to create the first map?" asked Tristan.

"You may either create it on paper or on computer," said Mr. Kishpaugh. "I have large white sheets on my desk if you want to do it by hand. The PDF of the maps I mentioned is on the homework portal, and I would utilize them extensively as you create your map. You are welcome to search online for more historical maps if you like, but please start with these. This is due Friday. Any other questions?"

When there were none, he said, "Get to work!"

Andrea said softly to Lucie under cover of the ensuing chatter. "What if that area marked *wolf* is important to our mystery?"

"I know!" said Lucie. "We have to figure out what it is ASAP."

They started poring over the maps, comparing current versions with the historical ones.

"Look, the *wolf* spot on the old map is west of Hoxit," said Andrea. "Look for something in the mountains with a river curving around it."

"Hey, here's Forests of Wolf, and it's west of Hoxit," pointed out Lucie. "Do you see Wolf Place anywhere?"

"No… Wait, yes! It's just at the base of this river," said Andrea excitedly.

"Follow the river up…" Lucie pulled the current year's map with her mouse. "It curves around this hill… and… Oh, my goodness!"

The two girls stared at each other. "Shuford Lodge!" they exclaimed together, and then they squealed and started jumping around.

"Hey, you pushed my stuff!" grumped Amy. She grabbed her stack of books and moved them exactly one inch back to where they had been, and then she straightened the corners of the stack to line up precisely.

"Sorry, Amy," giggled Lucie.

"It isn't funny!" protested Amy, casting the girls a dirty look and turning her back on them.

"Okay," said Lucie. Then she whispered to Andrea, "We were brought back full circle! We've got to find out more about Shuford Lodge!"

"You mean *Waya!!!*" corrected Andrea triumphantly. They sat down and buried themselves in their computers, digging for nuggets in the maps.

Near the end of the period, Andrea nudged Lucie. "We need to know more about Shuford Lodge, right?"

"Yeah," said Lucie. "But I looked at their website, and it only has an outline of the history of the place."

"So, we need to go there!" urged Andrea. "Can your mom take us? My mom and dad are working until later."

"No, she's got an appointment in Gainesville," said Lucie. "I'm supposed to go to Nana's today."

"Can your Nana take us?" asked Andrea. "I can text her."

"Try it. If she can, you can bike over to her house after school, or we can pick you up," said Lucie.

"What are you guys talking about?" nosed in Amy.

"Just research," said Andrea smoothly, pulling out her phone. "You got your map done?"

"Almost. I'm still working on the color-coding and integrating the layers," said Amy primly.

"Oh, yeah, we're right there with you," said Andrea, rolling her eyes as she texted Nana.

"Put the phone away, please!" Mr. Kishpaugh called from across the room.

"Yes, sir!" said Andrea, slipping her phone back in her book bag and giving Lucie a hidden thumbs-up.

After school, Lucie rode the bus to Nana and Pop's and found them waiting for her. They piled into Pop's car and drove over to the Longstreets' home, where they picked up Andrea. It was windy today, creating a bit of a chill in the air, so they came prepared with light jackets.

"Thanks, Mr. Stafford!" said Andrea as she hopped into the backseat with Lucie. "Where's your Gran?" she asked Lucie.

"She's taking it a little slow today, so she stayed home," said Lucie. "Nana called ahead to Mr. Roderick, and he said he could give us a tour, including the grounds. Gran already went on her walk this morning and thought she'd give it a miss."

Pop drove through Hoxit, the county seat of McCall County, regaling the girls with tales about some unusual deliveries in the area when he was working for the post office. They wound their way up the mountainous roads to Shuford Lodge, where they found a parking place near the front steps. There were very few cars in the lot, which they hoped meant it wasn't crowded inside. Mr. Roderick was on the front porch, adjusting some of the fall décor, and he came greet them as they mounted the steps.

"Welcome!" he said heartily.

"Thanks for having us," said Nana. "We appreciate your taking the time."

"Not a problem! It's been very quiet around here today. And these two young ladies were such a help with the Festival, I can't say no," he replied. "I understand you're interested in a tour with details?"

"Yes, sir," said Lucie. "We're studying the history of McCall County in Social Studies. We've looked at people who settled here as well as locations in the county that have had special meaning or influence. Andrea and I realized that though we've been here a lot, we don't know much about Shuford Lodge."

"I see. Well, I suppose the very place to start would be in the kitchen. Come on in," Mr. Roderick said, and he ushered them through the heavy oaken front door and down the central hallway to the kitchen in the back. It was dominated by a huge stone fireplace on one end of the room although the rest of the room had been remodeled and updated, which had made it the ideal place for Mrs. Martin to manage the baked goods at the Festival.

Mr. Roderick explained, "This fireplace was built by Timothy Shuford back in 1828. He was one of the early settlers of McCall County, except it was part of Habersham County at that time. He was a bit unusual compared to the other settlers, in that he did not come from Western North Carolina as most of the early ones did. Timothy Shuford came from Savannah, and the tale goes that he had been a sea captain. He'd spent some time in a tavern in Savannah and won the land grant off another man in a card game. He came up to scout the situation, to see if he was going to give up the life at sea, and when he found this tract of land, he was won over."

"What drew him to this specific spot?" asked Nana.

"Well, the memoirs of one of Timothy's grandchildren mention that he was especially drawn to the gentle slope of the hill, and the trees were significantly smaller than on most of the surrounding land. He thought that they would be easier to clear for building a home or planting crops. He also was drawn to the river at the base of the property," answered Mr. Roderick, motioning out the window. "He made the house a priority, working to make it sturdy, because he hoped to have a family. So, almost two hundred years ago he dug a generous cellar out of the red clay hill and built the beginnings of this house."

Andrea was leaning against the counters, listening intently. "What did he do to make money? You can't sail an ocean ship anywhere near here, even up the river," she said.

"Good question, Andrea," replied Mr. Roderick. "He loved the sloping land and the river on this tract, but farming for more than feeding his family was going to be somewhat problematic. So, he opened a country store at the bottom of the hill and became a merchant."

"I'm betting he was successful, if the house became what it is today," commented Pop.

"You said it, Mr. Stafford," said Mr. Roderick. "Timothy Shuford was very successful, using his skills as a trader to build his business and was able in time to expand, adding a substantial store in Hoxit. He married Tilda Cantrell, and their family continued in the merchant trade over several generations. Let me show you through the rest of the Lodge."

They followed Mr. Roderick through the large house, stopping to admire the current art displays in the front room. Pop, who had never been upstairs in the Lodge, marveled at the workmanship on the decorative woodwork in the upper hallway. Mr. Roderick even took them to the basement, pointing out the crack that had tripped Andrea on Festival day.

"You'll be glad to know, girls, that I've had estimates made on fixing the crack. Unfortunately, both companies think we'll have to jackhammer the floor in order to repair it. I'd hate to see this old stone floor ruined," he said ruefully.

"Isn't the Lodge on the Historical Register? There are guidelines for renovation and repair that are rather strict if it is," said Nana.

"Shuford Lodge has applied for the Historical Register, as some of the building is old enough to be listed," said Mr. Roderick. "But the Shufords made many renovations and additions over the years that changed too many original aspects of the house and took the Lodge out of consideration for the Register."

Lucie crouched down to touch the arrowhead in the stone floor, tracing it with her finger. As she followed the rest of the group up the stairs, she had the uncontrollable urge to yawn.

The tour continued outside with Mr. Roderick pointing out the original locations of the Shuford well and barn, and the girls got tickled when he explained just how far from the cabin the outhouses had been!

"Were the Shufords frightened they might meet a wolf on the way to the bathroom?" asked Andrea, laughing.

"A wolf?" puzzled Mr. Shuford. "Why would they be frightened of wolves?"

Lucie said quickly, "We just saw symbol for wolf on a map today in Social Studies. It looked like it was in this area of McCall County, and we didn't know why it was there." She stifled a yawn, appalled. Why was she so sleepy?

"Ah," said Mr. Roderick thoughtfully. "I can't say why that would be. I've never heard of wolves around here. Maybe they were here long ago. I think people see coyotes these days, but not wolves."

"Strike one," Andrea whispered to Lucie as he paused to consider where to go next.

"Let's head down to the river," Mr. Roderick suggested. "Part of the allure of this land grant for Timothy Shuford was the fact that it included some natural caves. Legend has it that some of his seafaring buddies would come to visit him and hide their loot in the caves."

"He was a secret banker?" said Nana, amused.

"You could call it that!" laughed Mr. Roderick. "The government certainly wasn't aware of it. And it was still a remote location, with this area so mountainous, and at that time remote from Hoxit. Wouldn't be many official visitors dropping by."

They tromped down through the pastures, past the corn maze and the area where the archery contest had been held, and then they slipped and slid a little getting down the steep slope to the river. Andrea noticed Lucie yawning.

"How can you be sleepy? The air is so brisk!" she teased.

Lucie looked worried. "I don't know. I wasn't even sleepy until we were in the basement, and Mr. Roderick was talking about fixing the floor."

Mr. Roderick led them along the riverbank and then across some rocky terrain, climbing until they came upon a group of big rocks. He grinned, and, pulling several small flashlights from the pockets of his windbreaker, he handed one to each of the girls.

"We won't go in, because there's no telling who's decided it might make a snug den, but you can use the flashlights to get a good peek," he told them.

As the girls shone their flashlights into the dark opening in the rocks, they smelled the earthiness of the floor, and the air wafted, damp and musty, toward them.

"You could take a nap in there!" joked Andrea to Lucie.

Pop asked, "Is there any truth to the rumor that Shuford's sailor friends shanghaied men?"

Mr. Roderick laughed. "Well, the official account is of course, if they did, Timothy Shuford had nothing to do with it. But he did come from Savannah, and a restaurant there still has the tunnel to the river that men were dragged through."

"What does 'shanghaied' mean?" asked Lucie.

"Shanghaiing was a form of kidnapping," explained Mr. Roderick. "Men would go into a tavern, have an ale or two which were secretly drugged, and when they woke up, they would be on a ship in the middle of the ocean. They'd have to work their way free, and they couldn't get off the ship until the voyage was ended, back at the original port. They could of course try to escape, but they'd likely be halfway across the world and no means of getting back home."

"That's slavery!" exclaimed Andrea.

"It is, absolutely," agreed Mr. Roderick. "Labor was in short supply, and ship captains were often desperate to get enough workers to complete their voyage. Many of them resorted to illegal means to get the hands they needed. Laws were passed to stop the practice, of course, but it was like closing the barn door after the horse escaped."

After Nana and Pop took a turn peeking in the cave, the group started back to the Lodge, slipping a bit again on the rocky terrain. Mr. Roderick and the Staffords walked in front, Pop helping Nana over the dicey bits. Lucie yawned again, an ear-splitting, whopper of a yawn.

Andrea grabbed Lucie's elbow. "Wait a minute. When did you say you suddenly got sleepy?"

"In the basement, when Mr. Roderick was talking about fixing the crack," said Lucie.

"When he talked about a jackhammer, you mean," said Andrea intently. "Could you be getting a dream?"

Lucie stared at her. "You think?"

"Could be," said Andrea. "Look, we'd better catch up."

The two girls began to hurry down the path, and rounding the curve they suddenly hit a particularly steep hill. Lucie lost her footing, and she landed on what became a mud slide! She couldn't stop herself tumbling, skidding, sliding down the slippery slope.

"LUCIE!" Andrea yelled!

Mr. Roderick, Nana, and Pop whirled, jumping aside just in time as Lucie barreled toward their feet. Too late, Pop tried to grab her, just as her head came smack into contact with an old fallen log. She saw stars, and then all went black.

11

London, England
1619

He was sprinting through the dark, dodging between horses in the street, ducking under a carriage stopped on the corner, then exploding out the other side. He was out of breath and sweaty despite the chill in the air. His chestnut hair flopped in his eyes as he pelted down an alley, and his pumping arms had only a second to push the hair away, leaving his vision clear again.

"BOY!" a deep male voice shouted behind him. He could hear the pounding feet growing closer, so he veered down another alley, gasping for air. It was to no avail, though, for he heard again, "STOP, BOY! In the name of His Majesty the King!" and a dark form filled the light that was his only escape between the buildings.

He stopped abruptly, unsure of his next move, and whipping around to look behind him, he felt a heavy hand on the back of his collar. He was moving again, only this time it was under someone else's power, and he struggled mightily to get free.

"Let me GO!" he shouted, and the second man from the alley ahead came forward to grab his arm and help the first get him under control. The overwhelming stench of onions rolled off them both.

"Stop your squirming, boy," one of the watchmen told him roughly. "His Majesty hath not the patience for the vermin of London, for which thou hath a great resemblance. Wild hooligan thou mayest be, but perchance we put a stop to your begging ways?" The two men half carried, half dragged him toward the street as he continued his fight for freedom.

There was a swirl of light and color, and Lucie saw the boy again...

He rode in a cart, shoulder to shoulder with other grimy teenagers. A small girl of about eight years sat on the bed of the wagon crammed up against his left foot, and another little boy, even smaller than she, leaned against his right leg. There were about fifteen children stuffed into the cart which was pulled by a pair of old nags that plodded their way through the London streets. Two guards, one holding the horses' reins and the other riding the rear, kept the children from bolting from their transport.

The little girl at his feet started to whimper.

"Where do they take us?" she asked. "I do be so cold." She huddled closer to his leg, seeking solace and warmth. He saw her shaking in her ragged dress, and when he looked forward past the guard, he saw the breath of the horses billowing out into the frigid air in clouds of white.

The teenager to his right nudged him. "Nathaniel, you were close enough to hear the warden talking. Where are we going?" he asked in a low voice.

Nathaniel said quietly into his ear, "Bridewell Prison, Nicholas."

The small boy below him started to cry.

"Why Bridewell, Nathaniel? Why throw us in with the criminals?" Nicholas asked. "We are orphans, runaways, some pickpockets, sure, but we are children!"

"I hear tell they are readying ships for the wilds of Virginia and mean for us to be on them. They have nary the room anywhere else to put us but Bridewell, and the ships must be prepared," explained Nathaniel.

Nicholas looked hopelessly out the back of the cart. "Virginia!" he muttered, aghast at their fate.

The dream changed again, and the colors came together once more into Nathaniel…

He lay in a hammock, one among many that swayed unceasingly as the sailing ship drove through the seas toward the New World. Girls and boys of all ages were packed into the mid-deck, whiling away the time until the next meal arrived.

A sailor opened the hatch above their heads and yelled down, "All ready to the deck!" He withdrew his head while one of the older boys called from down the line, "Nathaniel Tatum, your group goes this day!"

Nathaniel swung down smoothly from his hammock and stood, crouching to avoid hitting his head on the low ceiling. He and the others converged on the ladder, barely containing their excitement at the opportunity to go above. He slipped into line, and after a series of ladders, emerged on the deck of the ship, embracing the salt air and spray, replacing the stinky, unwashed smells from the mid-deck with fresh, sharp scents.

He moved to the bow, wanting to be as close to the action as possible without getting in the way of the sailors who climbed the rigging, pulled the sheets, shouted and grunted and used language saltier than the sea. Nicholas joined him, taking deep breaths of the briny air.

They sat on the deck, facing the open sea. Great gusts of wind blew in their faces, tousling their hair. It was blissful to be out of the dark belly of the ship.

"How much longer, until we reach Virginia?" asked Nicholas.

"I do not know. Seems as though we have been on this ship forever," replied Nathaniel. "I still cannot believe I will never see my family again."

"Or London," said Nicholas. "I have never lived outside of a city. I can care for a horse; there are many in London. But there are no cities where they are taking us."

"No doubt, it will be a long time before this is over," said Nathaniel. The ship's rise and fall over the waves was endless, as were the years of captivity that stretched before them.

The light swirled anew, and the kaleidoscope reformed.

Nathaniel was in the hold of the ship once more, peering out an open porthole with Nicholas, their faces pressed as close to the opening as possible. The ship was still, but it vibrated as footsteps pounded above them, the crew setting the ship to rights beside the dock.

"Captain William Ewen!" a booming male voice hailed.

"Cheney Boyce!" answered another. "It has been too long!"

The two men met on the dock, clasping hands and pounding backs in welcome.

"It has been two years since I arrived back in Virginia on the *George*, and here you are darkening our doors again! What do you bring this time?" asked Cheney Boyce, full of cheer.

"This trip, it is children," said Captain Ewen.

"Children!" Cheney Boyce sounded shocked. "Robbed a nursery, have you?"

"Not I," protested Captain Ewen. "I only sail the *George*. Their Lordships put the cargo on board."

"Did someone say children?" a light, feminine voice asked.

"Mistress Yeardley!" said Cheney Boyce. "A pleasant day to you."

"And to you, Master Boyce. But what is this about children?" she asked, balancing the basket on her arm.

"Master Ewen says their Lordships have put children on board his ship," said Boyce.

"Why do they send children?" asked Mistress Yeardley, sounding puzzled.

"Their Lordships say they are ridding the London streets of starving pests," said Captain Ewen. "They have cleared the streets of children, the homeless, beggars, even orphans. This is only the first group to be sent. They are come to serve masters here in Virginia."

"For how long?" asked Boyce.

Ewen shrugged. "That is not my concern. I only deliver the goods. Governor Yeardley will distribute them as he sees fit. Many will be useful for field work, but some are as young as eight years old. I have a hundred on board."

"A hundred children! And more to come!" Mistress Yeardley sounded shocked. "Separated from their parents, or those who could care for them? It has the sound of kidnapping! Are they indentured servants, or slaves?"

"I do not traffic in slaves, Temperance Yeardley!" insisted Ewen, his face turning red. "This was ordered by the authority of the King!"

"I do not know," said Boyce, shaking his head. "I wonder if the children had a voice in this matter. How criminal could they have been, to be shipped across an ocean to the unknown?"

"I am going to my husband!" cried Temperance Yeardley. "I have not heard even a whisper of this. Children!" She spun around, her heavy skirts flying, and took off down the dock toward Jamestown.

Inside the ship, Nathaniel looked at Nicholas. "Kidnapping, she says."

Nicholas gave him a long look. "I think she has the right of it," he said, and he turned away from the light.

"KIDNAPPED!" Lucie cried. Her eyes flew open to see Nana and Pop's faces over hers, with Andrea close by. "They were kidnapped!"

"Who was kidnapped?" asked Pop, bewildered.

"Whoever we're supposed to help," said Lucie loudly. "Kids, if it's like the dream."

"No, don't sit up," said Nana, as Lucie tried to move. Her head seemed to be resting on a rolled-up jacket or something. "Just rest easy. Who was in the dream?" she asked gently.

"Nathaniel Tatum and his friend Nicholas," said Lucie, starting to gesture excitedly. "Lots of children, on a ship, sent from England to Virginia. They were taken from the streets of London; Nathaniel was running, and he was grabbed by two big, smelly men. Come to think of it, lots of the dream was smelly," she mused.

"Nathaniel Tatum!" exclaimed Nana. "I don't remember much about him. We'll have to look him up when we get home."

"They were TAKEN, Nana!" cried Lucie, grabbing her arms. "Taken away from their families, from their homes if they had them, from everything that was familiar. Some of them were tiny kids, no older than eight years old! Nathaniel looked like he was Sean's age!"

"Hush, child," said Nana soothingly. "I know. But it was… wasn't Nathaniel Tatum in the 1600's? This was four hundred years ago."

"It doesn't matter that it was hundreds of years ago!" exclaimed Lucie. "Something like that happened here, and we have to find out what it was!"

"Do you think it had anything to do with Timothy Shuford? He was a ship captain," said Andrea.

"I dunno," said Lucie. "Maybe Mr. Roderick knows. Wait, where is he?" she asked, looking around.

"He went for a blanket," said Pop. "We wanted to keep you warm. You've been out for at least five minutes. He talked about calling 911, but Andrea let me know that you two thought an ancestor dream was coming, and we talked him into waiting, as well as into getting the blanket. We thought you might not want to advertise the ancestor dreams to him."

Lucie nodded, starting to calm down. "He's a nice man, but…" She trailed off.

"That's what we thought," said Nana, nodding. "Do you want to move now?"

Lucie sat up with her aid, realizing that Pop's jacket was spread over her legs, and Nana checked all over her head for a bump. "I thought sure you'd have a concussion, but you don't seem to have any evidence of one, either on your head or in your eyes. You look clear as a bell!" she marveled.

Mr. Roderick came rushing up, carrying a red plaid stadium blanket. "Lucie! You're conscious!"

"Yeah, Mr. Roderick. I'm really sorry to have been so much trouble," said Lucie ruefully.

"Oh, no! Not at all. Your tumble sure gave us a fright, though!" said Mr. Roderick. "Would you like to wrap this blanket around you?"

Nana intervened. "That would be lovely, Ken. Here, Lucie, let me help," she said, supporting Lucie as she stood up, handing Pop's jacket to him, and then bringing the blanket around Lucie's shoulders. Andrea retrieved her purple fleece jacket that had been under Lucie's head.

They started back to the Lodge, Pop holding on to Lucie's elbow and Andrea walking just behind her, though Lucie didn't think she needed the help.

"Mr. Roderick," said Andrea over her shoulder, "do you know of any tragedies, or disappearances, or anything, having to do with Shuford Lodge?"

"Why, no, Andrea," said Mr. Roderick, still sounding a little rattled from Lucie's fall. "Not that I can recall. The Shufords have a pretty typical history for people in this county, if you disregard the rumors of hidden treasure. Farmers, merchants, even some census takers sprinkled here and there. Nothing that would hit the newspapers. Why do you ask?"

"Oh, just wondering," said Andrea lightly. "You never know what might surface when you dig a little into history."

She quickened her step a little to walk close to Lucie. "Strike two," she said softly.

"But we're not out yet," said Lucie determinedly, watching her step very carefully.

12

Andrea and Lucie were in the high school cafeteria, eating pizza. They looked like fashion twins, in ponytails, jeans, and their new navy band t-shirts, only Lucie's jeans were her favorite paint-splashed ones. The place was crazy; seventh and eighth graders were talking at the top of their voices, cramming pizza into their mouths, guzzling soft drinks and waters. Section leaders from the high school band had been there at the start, to talk to them about marching band, but they'd just left to get dressed in uniforms for the football game.

Mrs. Brackley stood with the high school director, Mr. Laughner, who was a great teacher and an even better tuba player. Sean loved his jokes, especially when he started rolling with a whole series of puns. Mr. Laughner told people that with a name like his, he had to cultivate his funny bone.

Tristan ran up to their table. "Guys, guys, you gotta help me!" he cried. His red hair was standing on end.

"What's the matter, Tristan?" asked Andrea, popping the last bite of crust in her mouth.

"My phone is stuck in Spanish mode!" he said, shaking the phone in his hand.

"What do you mean?" asked Emily Carter.

"If I ask it for directions, it replies in Spanish. If I ask it to look something up on the internet, it replies in Spanish. If I search on my apps, the words are in Spanish!" he said, handing the phone to her.

Kelton and Tommy came up behind Tristan, trying to hold in their grins but failing utterly.

"How did this happen?" asked Lucie, leaning over to look at the phone while Emily tried to troubleshoot it.

"I left my phone on the table for just a minute when I went to get a cupcake, and when I came back, it was doing THIS!" Tristan was beyond distraught.

Andrea narrowed her eyes at Kelton and Tommy. "Did you guys see anyone messing with Tristan's phone?" she asked pointedly.

"Who us?" Tommy said, eyes wide with innocence. "No, didn't see a thing!" Kelton shook his head, too. Andrea, however, was not convinced.

"Hey, I got it!" Emily cried triumphantly. "It's all back in English now." She handed Tristan his phone. He started tapping immediately, and an expression of relief spread across his face.

"Gee, thanks, Emily! You're the best!" he enthused. He looked at their table. "Hey, do you want that brownie?" he asked.

Andrea rolled her eyes. "Boys!" she exclaimed. "Go ahead and have it," she told him. Tristan grabbed the brownie and stuffed it in his mouth, thumbs working overtime on his phone.

Just then, Mr. Laughner said something to Mrs. Brackley and left the cafeteria, headed in the direction of the band room. Mrs. Brackley clapped her hands for attention. When the volume had reduced to a murmur, she began to speak.

"Seventh and eighth grade band members, please be finishing your pizza and start cleaning up your space. Put all trash in the garbage cans and the water bottles in the recycle bin. We will move to the outer courtyard soon to join the high school band. Make sure you are wearing the McCall County Band t-shirt you were given tonight, as it is your ticket into the game. Eighth grade, you should have your instruments with you when you leave here. We will warm up outside with the high school."

The noise grew deafening again as the students started their exodus from the cafeteria. Amy Lucas recruited a seventh-grade cleanup crew, which was met with a few grumbles but reasonable participation. When all was set to rights, they gathered in the courtyard.

Mrs. Brackley looked her students over. "Cynthia Jones, where is your band t-shirt?" she asked.

Cynthia looked down at herself, seeing a white t-shirt emblazoned with a pink flamingo above her leggings, blinked, and grinned sheepishly. She dashed back into the cafeteria, emerging a few minutes later in the dark navy shirt everyone else was wearing.

After warm-up, the high school band formed a double line with the percussion in the middle. The eighth graders carefully held their instruments, grouped directly behind the color guard, and the seventh grade was next, bringing up the rear.

They set off for the stadium, marching to the cadence played by the drum line, and as they made a turn Lucie could see Sean up ahead. His shoulders were back, his trumpet held precisely as he marched in step. The deep navy blue of his uniform was accented with crisp white lines and gloves, and it was finished with a fluffy white plume atop his hat. Lucie thought he looked sharp.

They filed into the stadium and then split, the high school band going to the back sideline to assemble in their spots for their pre-game show, and the middle schoolers following Mrs. Brackley to the stands, finding seats in the band section. The bleachers were filled with supporters for both schools, and the Stephens County High School band was a large presence in the away stands.

The McCall County band marched out to perform pregame, and Mrs. Brackley looked around her, ensuring that all her students were facing the flag, hats off when the national anthem was performed. The hubbub of the crowd resuming, the band formed the tunnel for the McCall football team to run through full throttle in their white home jerseys, bursting through the paper banner held by the cheerleaders at the end.

As the two football teams regrouped on opposite sidelines, the announcer greeted the crowd. "Ladies and gentlemen, welcome to the Friday night contest between the Stephens County Indians and... YOUR McCall County Bears!"

The crowd roared! The game took off, with both bands playing constantly during breaks in the action. Lucie and Andrea were standing beside high school band members, wishing they had their instruments like the eighth graders so they could play, too.

The Indians of Stephens County were up 14-7 when the bands left the stands to get into position for their performances during half-time. The field looked incredibly busy, with the football game still being played, and two bands encircling it on the track. Lucie could see her dad amongst the prop crew, holding the front ensemble instruments and props back until the field was clear. Finally, the second quarter ended, and the Stephens County band converged on the field.

Lucie thought their red and black uniforms were very impressive, especially as a backdrop for the color guard uniforms. Each member of the color guard was dressed in bright colors, the girls with long, full skirts and the guys in dark pants with a tailored jacket. Their prop crew brought on several pieces of a low circular stage, which some of the band members hopped on and stood at attention.

"We have an extra treat tonight, football fans!" boomed the announcer's voice. "For your half-time entertainment, we have dueling Latin shows from two very fine marching bands! First up, the Stephens County High School Indian Marching Band presents *Los Conquistadores*, *The Girl from Ipanema*, *Chihuahua* and *Tio Macaco!*"

From the opening trumpet volley, Lucie was thrilled. She felt a shiver down her spine, and she enjoyed every minute of the show, from the excitement of *Los Conquistadores,* to the swaying *The Girl from Ipanema,* to the crowd joining in shouting "chihuahua" on the third piece, to the bouncing baseline in *Tio Macaco.* She loved how the color guard used their skirts as an extra accessory, extending them to each side like a Latin dancer would. They came off the field quickly at the end of the show, assembling on the front track and crouching down to watch McCall County march.

"Continuing the fun, ladies and gentlemen," said the announcer, "Please welcome the McCall County High School Band, with their own Latin show. Selections include *Encantata, Oye Como Va, Malaguena,* and *Hot Hot Hot!*"

Lucie had seen Sean march in this show several times, and she always waited for the trumpets and marching horns to wail it out on *Malaguena,* because it was Sean's favorite. He loved coming down the front sideline for their feature, and the Stephens County band was right there tonight, taking in the high-octave thrill up close and personal. They went wild, and the mood continued into the final movement.

The crowd had been on its feet in the stands since the middle of the Stephens County show, dancing to the music, and when McCall County hit *Hot Hot Hot!,* Lucie felt another shiver down her spine. She felt a thrill as the majorettes' special lighted batons whirled like red fireworks high above the band. She couldn't stop smiling or dancing in her spot. The student sections of both schools were shouting "Hot, Hot, Hot!" and the Stephens County Band was joining in from the track, barely able to keep from standing up and dancing themselves. The electricity in the air was infectious, and it continued as the football teams re-entered the stadium and started the second half of play.

Having put their instruments away, the two bands came together in an area off the track, grabbing snacks and drinks provided by the band boosters and renewing friendships from district events. Lucie found herself talking to one of the

Stephens County clarinet players, complimenting their show. She was really easy to talk to, explaining where they'd performed their show in competitions and even relating some of their woes.

"I mean, right when we went on the field at Norcross, rain absolutely dumped on us! And when we went to a competition at Winder, our generator went out for the electronics, you know, the computer we use for special sound effects. They had to run another generator to us, and we were almost late getting *Los Conquistadores* started on time! We could have lost points if we ran over our allotted time!" she exclaimed.

"What does *Los Conquistadores* mean?" asked Lucie.

"Oh, it's Spanish for *The Conquerors*," the clarinet player explained.

Lucie felt another shiver go down her spine, but she didn't know why. Andrea bounced up with Emily, and they peppered the Stephens County players with questions. Lucie didn't have a chance to get Andrea alone, so she had to keep the shivers to herself.

The bands returned to the stands for the fourth quarter, which had a very thrilling ending. The two teams were tied at the two-minute warning, and suddenly the Bears sacked the Indians' quarterback, causing a fumble. They were lucky to grab the football, as two McCall Bears were running over each other trying to scoop it and run to the endzone. Finally, one of them had the sense to fall on the ball, and with no penalties on the play, the Bears were in business. The Indians were able to hold them back from making a touchdown, but in the final ten seconds, the Bears lined up to kick a forty-yard field goal.

The spectators were screaming! Stephens County supporters were trying to distract the kicker, and McCall County fans were trying to out-do them with encouragement. Lucie held her breath... the kick was up... and good!!!

The McCall County band broke into the fight song, the football team was leaping across the field, and then the game was over. Lucie felt elated, and her eyes shone with excitement. As the stands emptied, she followed the rest of the band back to the band room where they put away their instruments. Then she and Sean went to the courtyard to find their parents.

"There you are!" came their mother's voice out of the crowd. The rest of her emerged, her honey-brown hair tucked into a baseball cap and a light jacket slung over her shoulders. She smiled at them both, enveloping them with warmth. "What a game! Your dad has the car over in the side lot, but we may never get out. Traffic is crazy tonight!"

She led them over to their minivan, and they all climbed in. "Laurel, you got a phone call while you were gone," said Rob, handing her cell phone to her. "We might as well stay here for a bit. There isn't much point in our leaving yet; it will be ages until we get out."

She checked her voice mail, listening intently. "Hey, it's Zimina," she said. "They've fired up the kiln. I took some of my pieces over earlier this week, and they're putting them in with theirs. She wondered if we'd like to go see the kiln in action tonight."

"Aw, Mom, I'm in my uniform," protested Sean.

"I'd like to see it," said Rob. "How about you, Lucie?"

"Sure!" said Lucie, still pumped from the night.

"Sean, there's Josh," said Laurel, watching people trickle through the parking lot and spotting their tawny-haired neighbor. "What if you catch a ride home with him?"

"That's good," said Sean, and he was out of the car before anyone else could speak, hailing Josh and his parents. After a quick consultation, Sean was back.

"They said no problem, Mom," said Sean. "I'm bushed. I'll see you at home?"

"You betcha!" said Rob, and Sean took off for Josh's car.

It did take a while to get out of the school parking lot, but as they moved slowly into line, Lucie could see the Stephens County band buses and equipment trucks still parked up near the stadium. She leaned her head back against the seat and thought about the night. Her dad waited his turn patiently, rolling down the window to thank the volunteer who had stepped out to direct traffic. Then he took them calmly and steadily through the curvy, mountainous roads to the Crack-Stackin' Pottery.

13

When they reached the pottery, Rob slid into a spot among several cars in the parking lot, and they walked around the building to the back. Lucie could feel the heat of the kiln as soon as they rounded the corner of the building, and there were lights trained from the building onto the open shed where the kiln was housed.

"Laurel!" exclaimed Zimina, straightening up from the front of the kiln. It looked like she had been adjusting some of the bricks. The gold in her braids shone in the firelight. "So glad y'all could make it!"

"Oh, we wouldn't miss it!" said Lucie's mom, hugging Zimina. "It never gets old, watching clay being forged by fire."

"Well, I wouldn't say that," chuckled Zimina. "Some days, I'd really rather put this thing on a timer and go get a snooze, myself. Instead, I'm here, moving bricks around, playing with the dragon!" She shook hands with Rob and smiled at Lucie. "Come on over and have a peek!" she invited.

They walked over to the rounded front of the kiln, and Zimina pointed to a hole in the bricks. "That's a spy hole," she said. "Laurel's pieces are over on the left side. Have a look."

Lucie's dad peeked in, taking a moment to adjust to the light. "Wow, that's really impressive!" he said, moving aside for Lucie to see. "Those pots are close together. How much space do you have to leave between them?"

"They need at least an inch between each one," said Zimina. "Then, about an inch and a half from the top to the next shelf. We do pack them in when we use this kiln."

Lucie looked in the spy hole. "What are those pointy things in there with the pots?" she asked.

"Those are pyrometric cones," said Zimina. "They tell us what the temperature is. We can't use a thermometer, so we use the cones. When the kiln reaches a specific temperature, the point on a cone starts to droop and curve over. We call it dropping the cone."

"Did the native potters use kilns, too?" Lucie asked.

"Oh, no," Zimina said, shaking her head. "They put the pots directly into the fire. They had to reinforce the clay with crushed shells and bone or sand to make the clay strong enough, but they surrounded the pots with open fire."

Lucie peeked in again. She located one of her mother's creations beside a pyrometric cone, and near it, one glowing face jug stood out, its eyes like black rocks, full of the power of the fire. Lucie felt like it looked straight at her, and she felt another shiver go down her spine.

She moved away from the spy hole and joined her dad a little removed from the heat. Her mom took her turn to peer in, and then she spent some time talking with Zimina while they moved around the kiln. Some of the other pottery employees were feeding the fire while Zimina was adjusting the bricks on the sides of the walls. Fire leapt in tongues out of the holes she made to let more oxygen into the kiln, and Lucie thought of her earlier comment. It did look like a huge mythical beast was housed inside, roaring to find its way out.

Lucie drew closer to her dad, and he put his arm around her. "Doing okay, Luce?" he asked.

She leaned into him. "Yeah, Dad," she said, sighing. "But I've been having some odd shivers tonight, and I'm a little… apprehensive," she said hesitatingly.

He squeezed her a little and said, "Apprehensive about what?"

She said, "There may be an ancestor dream coming, Dad, and I'm a little scared of it."

He reflected a moment and then said, "Well, have you ever been hurt in any of these dreams?"

"No," she said.

"Why does this one scare you?"

Lucie thought. "I guess my head thwacking into a log the last time has something to do with it," she admitted. "I've never been in any kind of danger before, when the dreams were coming."

Her dad said, "That's understandable." He paused, and then went on. "But you're having these dreams in order to help someone or something. Maybe tripping and falling into the log last time was an accident. You know one of your first dreams came quickly, the one at Nana and Pop's house. Maybe it was urgent that you got the message, or you were close to something that would trigger the message."

"I guess so," Lucie said.

"These dreams are a gift," said her dad warmly. "So, take it one step at a time and know that your mom and I are right here. Trust your ancestors, that they have good intentions to be of help."

He moved to stand behind her, wrapping his arms about her, and they stood together quietly, watching the team around the kiln. Lucie's mom was soaking in the creation of art, chatting with the workers. Lucie felt comforted, and a calm fell over her like a sprinkling of snow, soothing away both the excitement and uncertainty of the night.

Finally Laurel reluctantly pulled away from the kiln and came over to them, looking at her watch.

"I didn't realize how late it was getting!" she exclaimed. "I'm so sorry!" She took a closer look at the two of them, and her eyes zeroed in on her daughter.

"Lucie, what's happened?" she asked with concern.

Rob answered for Lucie. "We probably should get home soon. It would be good for her to be in her own bed when dreams come tonight," he said with a significant look, raising his eyebrows a little. Laurel's eyes widened.

"Let's get home then," she said, reaching out to touch Lucie on the arm. Calling goodbyes and thanks to Zimina and her crew, they moved quickly to the car and got in.

Lucie thought there was a chance she would fall asleep on the way home, since she'd had an ancestor dream in the car once before. But she was still wide awake when they reached home.

Carson was in the kitchen waiting for them, dancing around their feet in his excitement, and he was extremely thorough giving Lucie a good sniff. As a result, he didn't let her out of his sight while she got ready for bed, even though she gave him a huge rub all over, especially on the side of his head, which he loved. It was Lucie this time who gave Carson a boost onto her bed, and he kept a watchful eye as her parents came in to say good night. After scratching a bit on his fleece blanket, he finally lay down, and Lucie turned out the light.

Iredell County, North Carolina
February 1781

The silence was absolute. It surrounded the farm as completely as the mountains that rose to either side. There was no sound; no chirping of birds, no arguments of squirrels, no early croaking of frogs in the swamps.

She stood still as a statue, her feet rooted to the wooden plank floor. She was frozen, and every heartbeat thudded in her chest as through the kitchen window she watched her daughters and grandchildren disappear into the winter forest, slipping away across the marshy ground to safety. The last turned briefly, herself with a tiny baby strapped to her body in a shawl, looking back at the home that held the matriarch and center of their world. Then she, too, melted into the gray arms of the forest, bundled against the February chill.

They were coming. Word had reached them moments before, and she had made her quick decisions. She knew a fight was eminent and could not be avoided. So, when she heard the pounding of hooves, the war cries of men, a cacophony of sound, she turned on her heel and walked to the front door of her house, the home her husband and sons had built with their sweat and blood. She watched out the front window and waited for their next move.

Their green coats were covered in dust, their sweaty horses stomping and pulling at their bits, wanting water and feed and rest. One man swung down from his horse and approached the steps of the house. She opened the door and stood with dignity, staring at this trespasser on her land.

"Mistress Brevard? Wife of John Brevard?" the officer asked, his attitude assured and challenging, his hair tousled and wild.

"I am Jane Brevard," she replied. "My husband is John Brevard, but he is not at home at present."

"We'll catch up with him, I imagine. Your son-in-law was General William Lee Davidson?" the officer continued his query.

Jane stared at him with steely eyes. "Yes, General Davidson was my daughter Mary's husband," she affirmed.

"One of our boys got him good at Cowan's Ford," the officer bragged, and the unruly men behind him began to guffaw. "The Redcoats tried, but it took a Tory to bring that man down."

She would not let him see weakness. She would not even respond. She simply stared.

"Yessir, that was a windfall for us, taking that fella out. Heard his wife had just had a baby. Such a shame, that wee one never knowing its pa," the green-coated man goaded her, the men behind him jeering and poking each other in glee.

"What is your business on my land?" she cut into their laughter with a voice like ice.

"Why, ma'am, it's simple," the officer spread his hands wide, mocking her. He pulled a paper out of his pocket and unfolded it. "Says here, we're to burn every building on the place."

She was rooted to the floor again, but this time, she could hardly breathe.

He put his booted foot on the steps to her home, leaned in, and said softly, tauntingly, "Yes, ma'am. We're to burn the lot. And best of all, you get to watch." He turned to his men and yelled, "Dismount, boys, and get the party started!"

As the men whooped and hollered, swinging down from their horses, leading them to trees and tying them securely, she found her voice. "Why? Why in the world would you do such a thing?" she cried.

The officer, his foot still on the step, looked at her and said mockingly, "Why, ma'am, you have eight sons in the rebel army. His Majesty King George just can't have that, now can he?" He smiled sneeringly, then left the steps of her home to join his men as she stared at them, furious, unbelieving, aghast.

"You will not!" she cried. "I will not let you!"

She spun on the spot, intent on getting some kind of weapon—her husband and sons had taken the guns—when two men approached her and roughly pulled her off the porch, hauling her over to where their horses were tied, and one of them stayed, his strong hands holding her prisoner, forcing her to watch the destruction of her home as she wrestled and fought to get away.

The men spread out like ants across her farm, gathering wood, building a bonfire, throwing her family's possessions into the mud and trampling on them. They turned the animals out of the barn, the pig sty, and the chicken house, and the terrified animals made the chaos even worse, running every which way while they tried to escape the pandemonium of wild men.

The bonfire did not have to be very large for the men to light their torches, and they started setting fire to the buildings. First the barn, the smokehouse, the summer kitchen, and the storage buildings were lit. They even set fire to the outhouse. The chill of the February air went unnoticed in the blaze of heat that rolled through the clearing as if from an open oven door. Then the Tories turned their attention to the house, setting their torches at the four corners and standing back, wanting to make the pain of her loss stretch out even longer.

She watched in horror and amazement until she could take no more, and then she wrenched herself away from her captor and ran back into the house. She grabbed anything she could, filling her apron and arms, running down the steps and dumping her load on the ground. The men laughed, watching her, and when she had made another trip, dragging a rocking chair out onto the porch as the flames licked the sides of her house, one of the Tories ripped it out of her hands and threw it back through the front door. She did not give up but ran in again and again, trying to save anything, staying close to the floor, peering through the smoke. But every time she emerged from the blaze, they would grab her precious memories and throw them back into the flames.

Finally, as the house was engulfed in the inferno, one of the men grabbed her arms once more and held her back, forcing her to stop, forcing her to watch, forcing her to live.

The Tories stood there, chatting casually with each other, making jokes, eating food they had packed for the trail, and feeding their horses while they basked in the glow of their destruction. When they were satisfied that the job was done, they mounted their horses around her still form. The commander wheeled his horse around, giving her a mock salute before spurring his horse to the front of the company and galloping away at the head of the thundering whirlwind of green.

She stayed in silence until the fires wore themselves out, finished with any morsel of wood or fragment of cloth they might consume. She waited until the tall structures which until hours ago had held her life were reduced to mere ashes, and then she haltingly started to walk. There was no use in trying to find the livestock, as the noise and the stench of smoke would have driven them far away. There was nothing to save now, except what actually mattered the most.

She walked toward the winter forest where, hours ago, her loved ones had escaped from the danger. She walked, one foot in front of the other, her eyes determined, toward her family. The men would come home from the war—oh, they would, wouldn't they?—her breath caught; she would not cry! She kept walking, stealing between the trees, her feet and skirts rustling the dead leaves. One foot quicker, another, another, until she was running, running to find them. This would not stop them from their cause for independence and liberty. Together, they would rebuild. Together, they would survive. Together, they and their country would triumph!

Lucie found herself sitting up in bed in the moonlight, her body wracked with sobs, tears streaming down her face. Carson crept across the bed to her, crawling into her lap. She wrapped her arms around him, and they sat together, his body pushed against her in sympathy, until the agony was spent. Her breathing returned to normal, her muscles began to relax, and she hugged her dog, looking up into the sparkling heavens, mulling over what she had just seen.

14

The next day, Lucie stood in her parents' workshop, hands on hips, her hazel eyes staring at the big stand-up whiteboard her dad liked to use when he was figuring out math problems. She'd chosen a bright yellow crew shirt and her comfy overalls today, the ones with a unicorn on them, and her honey-brown hair was pulled back in a messy bun.

Carson sat quietly at her feet, also looking at the whiteboard. Lucie had a determined gleam in her eye and a burgundy dry-erase marker in her hand. She'd chosen it deliberately; black was too stark, yellow was too light, but burgundy erased well and could be seen easily.

She was waiting for the rest of her team to arrive. As soon as she woke this morning, she'd rushed to tell her family about the dream from Jane Brevard. They'd picked it apart and decided what to do next, which was to get Andrea, Nana, Pop, and Gran over as soon as possible. Lucie had called Andrea, and her mom had gotten Nana on the first try. Lucie had been planning on spending the day at

Andrea's before the dream came, but Andrea was adamant that they work on the mystery instead.

Carson's ears sprang up as Sean walked in the door, lugging a few folding chairs. "Mom said we might need these," he told Lucie.

"Have she and Dad left yet?" asked Lucie, still staring at the whiteboard.

"Yeah, they had to get going," said Sean. "They almost didn't, though. They wanted to stay and see how the mystery unfolds."

"I know," said Lucie, "but they had to go. This was one of the only weekends you didn't have a marching contest, and Dad said they'd chaperone the photography club trip to the State Botanical Gardens in Athens today. They can't let them down."

"You know there's nothing written on the board, right?" asked Sean, looking from Lucie to the whiteboard to Carson.

"Yup," said Lucie briefly. Carson blinked.

"LUCIE!!!" yelled Andrea from the driveway. She came barreling into the workshop and grabbed Lucie in a huge bear hug. Her tie-dye t-shirt dress billowed out around her black leggings, and her dark hair flew every which way. "Aiiiigggggghhhh!!!!" Barking, Carson jumped on them both, his floppy brown ears soaring as his short legs bounded off their bodies.

"Dude, chill," said Sean, ducking out of their way as Andrea swung Lucie around.

"I can't believe it!" said Andrea, ignoring Sean. "Another dream! We've got to figure this out!" She let go of Lucie and faced the whiteboard. "When do we start?"

"I think now would be a good time," said Gran as she stepped through the door looking fresh in a deep-rose ensemble. Pop and Nana were close behind her, and Carson rushed at the group. "Settle down, Carson. Lucie, come give me a hug," she said.

As Lucie did so, she felt a special pressure in Gran's embrace, as though she were giving her a little extra love without having to say it out loud in front of everyone. She looked up into Gran's face, and Gran gave her a quick wink. Lucie squeezed back.

"All right, then," said Gran briskly, releasing Lucie and pulling up a chair. "Let's get to it."

"Okay," said Lucie. She wrote Shuford Lodge at the top of the whiteboard. "We know that our mystery has something to do with Shuford Lodge. I think we should list everything we know, either from research or dreams, and then decide if we can see any patterns."

"Good plan, Lucie," said Pop. "What do we know that directly connects to Shuford Lodge?"

"The first thing we found was the arrowhead," said Andrea. "That big crack in the basement floor, and the arrowhead."

Lucie wrote Crack and Arrowhead on the left side of the board, Carson pacing beside her.

"Don't forget that lady with the jelly jars," reminded Sean. "What was her name?"

"Carmen Littlegalle," said Lucie, and she wrote the name on the board as well.

"Yeah, she acted really weird, just like Zimina did at the pottery museum," said Andrea. "She said they were cousins."

Lucie wrote Zimina and Cousins on the board, too.

"We've got pirates, treasure, caves, and kidnapping as possibilities," put in Pop. "Okay if I add them, Lucie?" He grabbed a green marker to match his Appalachian Trail t-shirt and wrote those words on the right of the board.

Nana spoke up. "Start another column, Lucie, for the native clues. Munsee and waya both mean 'wolf', don't they? And you found the Cherokee symbol for wolf on the map in the area of Shuford Lodge. So, wolf, waya, Munsee, beloved place, warning...?"

Lucie added them to the board, saying, "Do you think it was just a coincidence that the football game last night was against the Stephens County Indians?" Carson happened to step on her foot after she spoke.

"At this point, I'm not discounting anything," replied Nana, her eyes laser-beam focused on the board. "Is there more to add under natives?"

"The pottery museum had a lot about native pottery in it," said Lucie, looking at her, "and the dream from Julianna had the native potter, making a pot with wolf heads for spouts."

"The museum also had pictures and information about the native mounds found in Georgia," said Andrea. "Zimina kept talking about those, how they were found in groups of mounds, near running water, and were used for ceremonies and cultural centers."

Pop wrote Pottery, Mounds, and Ceremonies up on the board. "There's a river curving around the Shuford Lodge property," he commented, and added Running water to the list. He had to avoid Carson as he stepped back.

"Come here, Carson," invited Gran. Carson walked over, wagging his tail, and leaned into Gran's hand as she rubbed his head.

"Now, let's see. Nathaniel Tatum's dream was partly on a ship, right? And Timothy Shuford was a ship's captain," said Nana.

Pop wrote Ship and Ship Captain on the board.

"Tell us again about last night's happenings, Lucie," requested Gran. Carson laid down close to her feet.

Lucie ran through the evening with them again, mentioning Tristan's phone, the football game thrills, the shivers at the kiln, and the momentous, fiery dream.

"So," said Sean, "we've got Spanish, Conquerors, and Fire to add to the board."

Lucie did so, adding Hot, Hot, Hot and Bravery to the list as well.

"How about Dastardly Rascals?" said Pop with a grin.

"Yes!" cheered Andrea. Pop added them with a flourish.

Lucie stepped back and looked at the board.

"Wait," said Sean. "You said the Nathaniel Tatum dream came after a jackhammer was mentioned."

"We've got to put that in!" cried Andrea, grabbing the marker from Lucie and adding Jackhammer to the bottom. "That one was a warning!"

"I doubt someone in the past was dealing with an actual jackhammer," said Gran dryly.

"No, Mrs. Culwen!" said Andrea, whirling to look at her. "I bet they were telling us NOT to jackhammer!"

"Is that it, then?" asked Sean.

"Is what it?" asked Andrea.

"There's something under the Shuford Lodge that needs to be protected? Something native?" he said.

They all looked at the board, sorting the words in their minds, shifting them around.

Lucie said slowly, "We found the symbol waya on the old map in the location of the

Shuford Lodge. Nanichi, the native boy in New York, told Johannes that a place beloved to his tribe, the people of the wolf, was threatened, and it was in the mountains near a river. Thomas Chambers said the English were looking to clear small hills for settlement. Zimina was talking about native mounds," and she paused, then went on.

"Is it possible the hill that the Shuford Lodge is built on was a native ceremonial mound? Belonging to the people of the wolf, of this area?" She blinked, surprised.

"Oh, dear," said Gran. "What did they do?"

"How did they not know?" asked Andrea, aghast.

Pop said, "Ken Roderick said that the grandchild of Timothy Shuford wrote that he was drawn to the 'gentle slope of the hill' with smaller trees, easier to clear for a homestead. If the mound had been abandoned for some years, it could have been grown over."

"But why would they leave it?" asked Andrea.

"There's your answer," said Sean, walking up to the board and tapping it. "Conquerors. Spanish. Kidnapping. Fire. Hot, Hot, Hot."

Carson gave a faint whine.

"Oh, Sean, do you think?" asked Nana.

"Does he think what?" asked Lucie, her head turning from one to the other.

"He means de Soto," said Pop, looking grim.

"Hernando de Soto?" asked Lucie.

"The one and the same," said Pop. "Andrea, you got your phone with you?"

Andrea pulled it from the pocket of her dress. "Sure do. What do you need?"

"Look up Hernando de Soto, add Georgia to the search," he requested.

Andrea started tapping, and after a few websites that didn't help much, she hit gold.

"In the mid-1500's, Spanish explorer Hernando de Soto and his seven hundred men marched through the southern part of what became the United States, killing and looting, kidnapping and stealing. They had no supply chain, so they took what food they could find and demanded more from communities they came across on their way. They came through North Georgia on their return route as they headed back west to the Mississippi River," she reported.

"They weren't the only ones," said Nana. "There were a few more expeditions after de Soto's, and they caused as much havoc as his did. They were also great spreaders of disease, those Europeans."

"So, we're thinking that a native community, with a ceremonial mound..." said Lucie.

"A BELOVED, SACRED mound!" said Andrea excitedly, pointing at the board.

".... was attacked by a Spanish army?" asked Lucie, wide-eyed.

"And it was burned?" exclaimed Andrea.

"That would explain why the trees were smaller than those in the surrounding land," commented Pop. "They would have started growing again as the forest reclaimed the land that was decimated."

"People were kidnapped, too?" asked Lucie, dismayed by the revelations.

Nana nodded. "The Spanish explorers killed many natives and took those they didn't kill with them as slaves."

They all looked at each other, dumbstruck.

Sean was the first to break the silence. "How are we going to prove this? Or get someone to believe us?"

Gran sighed deeply. "I think, as distasteful as it is, I'm going to have to make a phone call." Carson stood up and shook himself mightily.

"To whom, Mother?" asked Nana.

"To Emmett Prendergast," said Gran. She had a look on her face as though she had smelled something rotten in the trash.

"Oh, dear," said Nana in her turn. She sat down in a chair and pulled her phone out of her purse. "Do you have to?" she asked Gran.

"I think it's the only way," said Gran, nodding.

"What?" asked Andrea. "Isn't he the man that told us about face jugs, after the lightning made you scream, Lucie?"

"Yeah," said Lucie, mystified. "Why do we need to call him?" she asked.

"Emmett Prendergast is a self-proclaimed expert on many aspects of North Georgia history," said Gran with some acrimony. "He and I have butted heads many a time. But the truth is, in his younger days he spent time in the Middle East on archaeological digs, and he met his wife there. His youngest son Graham followed in his footsteps, getting several degrees in archaeology. I'd be willing to bet that we could get them to Shuford Lodge if Graham's in town. We'll have to think of a good story that won't give Lucie's dreams away, though," Gran said.

"Don't archaeologists use satellite imaging now, to identify unnatural formations that could be man-made?" asked Pop.

Andrea's fingers started tapping again. "This website says they do," she reported.

"What if we mention satellite views on apps in connection with the map the girls found?" suggested Pop. "Say they were putting two and two together for their social studies project, and coupled with their recent visits to the Lodge, they wondered if there might be more to discover."

"That might do it," said Nana, nodding. "Mention, too, what Timothy Shuford's grandchild wrote in the memoirs about the small trees. It might intrigue him."

"I'll have to call someone for his number," said Gran. "But I think we can finagle this without too much difficulty."

In the end, Gran pulled it off beautifully. She was pleasant without being falsely gushy, gave enough information to whet Emmett Prendergast's appetite for a potential find, and didn't utter a whisper about Lucie's dreams or shiver feelings. When she finally disconnected the call, she was smiling smugly, and the girls were dancing around her.

"You did it?" they asked, and when she nodded with satisfaction, they yelled, "She did it!! She did it!!" and hugged her between them. Carson was barking again.

"Now, now," she said modestly when they calmed down. "It really wasn't hard to do. Emmett said his son Graham does happen to be visiting, and they were both intrigued, if a bit skeptical, about the possibility of Shuford Lodge having some archaeological discoveries lurking beneath it. But he suggested we meet them at the Lodge early this afternoon, since Graham is going home tomorrow."

"We should call Ken Roderick, then, and see if we can come to the Lodge," said Nana, looking concerned.

Gran handed her the phone. "See what magic YOU can do," she told Nana.

After looking up the number to the Lodge, Nana was on the phone with Mr. Roderick quickly.

"Hi, Ken," she said. "Nan Stafford here. Listen, I know it's a bit unusual, but we'd love to come back over to the Lodge this afternoon. The girls have done more on that social studies project, and they're wondering if there might be more to discover."

She listened for a moment. "Yes, that's right. And Emmett Prendergast would like to come too, with his son Graham… Oh, super, Ken, thanks so much. We'll see you soon," she said, and disconnected the call.

She looked at the rest of the team. "We're in!" she said, tossing her bright hair in triumph and smiling. "Let's grab some lunch on the way, have a picnic on the grounds, and then when the Prendergasts get there, we can get to work."

"But wait," protested Andrea, pointing at the whiteboard. "How do Carmen and Zimina fit in?"

Nana did a double-take at the board. "Ummm," she said, looking mystified. "Banks, any ideas?"

"Nope," said Pop.

"Me, neither," said Sean. "Maybe they were just having a bad day."

"No way," declared Andrea. "There is something going on there."

"Well," said Gran, "we'll have to figure it out. One step at a time, though, huh?" She headed for the door, Carson at her heels.

15

Sean and Lucie put Carson securely in the house, and Andrea went with them, calling her dad at his shop, Choestoe Antiques. As she filled him in on their conclusions, Sean suddenly realized they needed a bigger car to get them all to Shuford Lodge. Since Chu Longstreet had help at the shop, he was able to join the quest, and he arrived quickly, picking up Andrea, Sean, and Lucie while Pop drove Nana and Gran in his car.

The two cars stopped briefly in Hoxit for sandwiches at Dagwood's Sub Shop, and then they began to wend their way up to Shuford Lodge. Lucie thought they would never get there. She was on pins and needles, ready to unravel the mystery, and she was certain she couldn't even eat a bite of lunch. Andrea was drumming on the car seat beside her, full of nervous energy as well.

When they'd parked at the Lodge, the girls were the first out of the car, grabbing the bags of subs as they went. Andrea's dad Chu Longstreet and Sean were each balancing a cardboard drink caddy and bags of chips while Nana helped Gran out of the car.

Pop asked, "How about the picnic tables over by the old well?"

Lucie and Andrea veered in that direction, and Lucie was glad it wasn't too far to go. She didn't want to get too far away from the parking lot, so she could see when the Prendergasts got there.

"Who got the Italian sub?" asked Andrea, pulling sandwiches from her bag.

"I did!" said Pop, accepting it with satisfaction.

"Mine's the meatball sub with extra cheese," put in Sean.

"Dad, what did you get?" asked Andrea, face buried in the bag.

"I've got the roast beef with extra jalapenos and banana peppers," said Chu, catching an amused look from Nana. "Hey!" he laughed at her. "I like spice in life!"

"And in your belly!" Nana retorted. "Lucie, what are you doing?" she asked, diverted.

Lucie had been craning her neck, trying to see if anyone had arrived. "Oh, nothing," she said and started unloading her bag as well.

By the time lunch was finished, she realized she'd been wrong that she couldn't eat anything. Somehow her sandwich had disappeared without her noticing, except for her having slightly sticky fingers. She hadn't paid much attention to the chatter around her, though, so focused was she on the task to come.

Finally, a car came slowly up the drive. It stopped halfway up for a few minutes, and then it resumed its way to the parking lot. Emmett Prendergast emerged from the car, and he clumped over to their table, his cane helping him on the uneven ground.

"Well, look at you all, stuffing your faces," he said. "Nice day for a picnic, what?"

"Yes, it is, Emmett," said Gran. "Won't you join us?"

"No, no, it's time to get this show started," said Emmett. "My word, Nan Stafford, you look like an eggplant!"

Nana looked down at her sleeveless, vivid purple blouse. It gathered at the sparkly neck, and its silky material flowed down below her waist.

"Why, thank you, Emmett. That was just the effect I was going for," she replied dryly.

"Hmph," he said. "You about finished?"

Lucie was shoving lunch trash into bags as he spoke. "Did your son come with you, Mr. Prendergast?" she asked.

"Yes, yes, he got out halfway up the drive," said Emmett testily. "Come on, let's get a move on." He noticed Andrea's dad amongst the group. "Well, Chu, how are you? I didn't know you were with this crowd," he said.

Chu was amused again, his eyes twinkling in his round, coppery face. He wiped his mouth on a napkin. "Just keeping them in the middle of the road, Emmett," he said. "This is my daughter, Andrea. She's part of this investigative team."

Emmett snorted. "Investigative! I like that," he said with some contempt.

Gran bristled a little, but Emmett didn't see her as he had turned to head back to the parking lot. The group finished tidying up the table and followed him.

"Why did Graham get out of the car down there, Emmett?" asked Pop just as a dark-haired, olive-skinned man came into view. He wore a backpack and was pushing something that looked a little like a small lawn mower, but his head was bent over a box in his hand.

"He wanted to get readings in less-developed areas," said Emmett, watching. "We looked at the satellite images on his tablet, and it's possible we may find something. But anything immediately under the parking lot area would have been disturbed by construction."

Graham made his way to them, pushing his little wheeled contraption. "Well?" demanded his father as he handed the car keys to Graham. The two looked so different, thought Lucie, with Mr. Prendergast so gray and grizzly and Graham so tan and self-possessed.

"I think you may be on to something," said Graham, looking at the group. "Now, who's brainstorm was this?"

"Ours!" said Andrea. "Lucie and I have been working on a project for social studies."

"Well, good show, ladies," said Graham. "Why don't you all come over here to the side of the Lodge and see what I'm seeing."

He crossed the parking lot, pushing his contraption away from the picnic tables, and when he reached grassy lawn once more, he flipped a switch. The machine started humming.

"What is this?" asked Sean, circling around it.

"It's ground penetrating radar," replied Graham. "or GPR for short. It's like x-raying the ground. I can detect objects on my screen, see, through the layers of earth. The GPR sends electromagnetic waves into the ground, and the longer the time it takes for the wave to bounce back to the surface, the deeper the object is. It indicates the size and shape of the objects as well."

They each took a turn looking at the screen, seeing dark shapes every so often as he pushed it across the ground, keeping it as level as possible. He seemed to get more excited as they went along, but he wasn't giving much away. They watched Graham quietly for a while, and then Lucie asked him, "Can you take the machine indoors?"

"I can, if the space is big enough," he said. "But I also have a hand-held unit if needed."

Ken Roderick emerged from around the side of the Lodge and made his way over to them. "My goodness, Nan Stafford, you've brought a whole bevy of people with you!" he exclaimed, arms spread wide.

"I know, Ken, it's getting bigger and bigger," she replied. "You know Chu and Graham, don't you?"

"Absolutely!" Mr. Roderick said, shaking hands with them. "I haven't seen you in quite a while, Graham."

"I've been away on an archaeological dig," said Graham. "I'm headed back home to Charlotte, actually. Just stopped to see Dad on the way. I hope you don't mind that I've got my GPR running. It seemed too good an opportunity to pass up, since I had it in the car already."

"No problem at all," said Mr. Roderick. "So, what are we looking for, exactly?" he inquired.

Lucie took a deep breath. "Mr. Roderick, Andrea and I wondered if any native artifacts might be buried under the Lodge. Some of our research was leaning that way, and Mr. Prendergast said he might be able to help."

"Ah," said Mr. Roderick, still looking a little mystified. "Okay. What is your equipment saying, Graham?"

"I'd rather not say for sure yet," said Graham. He looked at Lucie. "You mentioned indoors, Lucie. Was there a specific reason?"

"Um, yes," said Lucie, exchanging a quick glance with Andrea. "There's an arrowhead buried in the basement floor, and… a big crack… and…

we think it would be a good idea to scan that area, too," she said, ending in a rush.

"Absolutely!" piped in Andrea, nodding.

"No, no," disagreed Emmett. "We'll have more luck out here. We avoided the parking lot because the land would have been disturbed; we should avoid the house, too." He gave the girls a grumpy look.

"Mr. Prendergast, I really think it's important," protested Lucie.

"Young lady, there is no reason to take this thing down there," said Emmett sternly. "Timothy Shuford dug that cellar. Anything there will be gone."

"I disagree, Dad," said Graham, quietly turning off his GPR. "Remember the church in Jamestown, Virginia? Archaeologists have discovered a treasure trove of historical artifacts under the basement floor there. It doesn't hurt to give it a try, if Mr. Roderick is agreeable." He smiled mildly.

"Ah, well, sure," said Mr. Roderick. "Come right this way."

He led the way back to the front steps and through the Lodge. The steps to the basement creaked with so many feet on them at once, and Graham was carrying the GPR as well.

It was a little crowded when all nine of them made it down into the basement. "For the GPR to have enough room to work, we'll need to spread out a little," said Graham.

"I'll open the doors to the storage rooms," said Mr. Roderick. "We can stand in the doorways while you work."

They sorted themselves out of the way, with Lucie, Sean, and Andrea perching on the stairs to get a clear view. Graham settled his equipment and turned on the power. He ran the GPR over the floor slowly, spending a lot of time on the big crack in the floor. When the GPR hummed over the arrowhead, he said, "Curious."

Chu Longstreet asked, "What's curious?"

Graham shook his head. "This arrowhead. It's not as thick as I expected it to be. It's like it's been completely flattened by something, run over and squashed."

Lucie and Andrea looked at each other, startled. "Like Emily's trombone!" whispered Andrea.

"I'm also seeing shapes that look like pottery, some of them intact with spouts," Graham said. "They are very close to the surface, for me to see them this clearly."

He moved the GPR near the doorways, and as it crossed the threshold of the face jugs room, he jumped. "Whoa!" he exclaimed.

"What is it?" asked his father excitedly.

"Come look, Dad," he said. "Is this what I think it is?"

They all waited with bated breath for Emmett to look at the monitor. He stared at it for a long while, and then he exchanged glances with his son. "You may be right. But there's no hint in the histories for this location."

"What?" burst out Andrea.

"Hold on a minute," said Graham. "I'm almost done."

He finished surveying the room and turned off the GPR. "Mr. Roderick, tell me about this floor," he said.

"We've been meaning to have it repaired for some time, but it was only recently that I brought in companies to give repair quotes," said Mr. Roderick. "Both of them recommended jackhammering the floor out and replacing it. I hate to do that, though."

"Is the Lodge on an historical registry?" Graham asked.

"No," said Mr. Roderick. "Too many changes have been made to the house by the Shuford family through the years to qualify."

"Hmm," said Graham. "Well, that may change soon. And, rest your mind at ease, there will be no jackhammering."

"I'm sorry?" said Mr. Roderick.

Lucie held her breath.

"I believe that beneath this floor, beneath this hill, is a find of great historical significance," said Graham. "The GPR has revealed object after object buried here, and I think we may very well have a native temple mound under us."

Mr. Roderick gaped at him. Andrea grabbed Lucie, and Sean clapped his hand on her shoulder.

"How? What?" Mr. Roderick sputtered.

"You're sure, Graham?" growled his father.

"Yes, Dad, I'm sure," replied Graham.

"I'd like to believe it, but there's nothing in the history of the county to suggest it," argued Emmett again.

"There may be nothing in the history from the time the Europeans came," said Chu gently. "But the Cherokee have many legends, some going back to the time of the Mississippians. We carry their stories with us, too."

"Any stories about ceremonial mounds?" asked Emmett skeptically.

"I am of the wolf tribe, and this section of the county has always held the deep respect of my people," said Chu. "We have lost the reason why, and so some have turned that respect into fear."

"Dad, can you go get my kit bag and brushes from the car?" asked Graham diplomatically, handing him the keys as his father began to bristle at Chu's words. "Get a soil sample or two if you will from farther down the hill on your way back, if you don't mind."

"Here, young man, you come help me," ordered Emmett with ill grace, creaking up the stairs and motioning to Sean, who followed him.

"Mr. Roderick," began Graham.

"Call me Ken, please," Mr. Roderick interrupted him.

"Okay, Ken," said Graham, "Some of the flooring around the crack seems to be loose."

"Yes, the contractors were testing it for their quotes," said Mr. Roderick.

"Would you object to my inserting some instruments into the crack?" asked Graham. "None should do any harm, and they may give us a more comprehensive picture."

"Not at all," said Mr. Roderick.

Everyone waited, chatting quietly, for Emmett and Sean to return. When they did, Graham pulled a probe from his bag and inserted it into the crack. When he pulled it out, he had a sample of the earth below. Then he compared his sample to the ones his father had taken.

"Just as I suspected," said Graham. "The samples support my theory. The evidence is much clearer on the samples from outside the house, but there are distinct traces in here, too. Beneath us, we have a layer of earth, but underneath it is ash, and then earth, red clay again."

"Ash?" burst out Emmett. "Ceremonial mound... Ash..." His eyes widened. "Conquistadors!"

Graham nodded. "I think so, Dad."

"What?" Mr. Roderick was lost again.

Nana explained. "Ken, if you've got a Mississippian mound under the Lodge, it's very possible that Timothy Shuford built on it because it had been grown over for hundreds of years. And the reason it was abandoned was that Spanish explorers burned the village and carried away the people as slaves."

Mr. Roderick wobbled a bit. Pop grabbed a chair and scooted it forward, easing Mr. Roderick into it.

"What," sputtered Mr. Roderick. "What do we do? What will the board of directors say? What will happen to the house? And the grounds?" He was completely kerflummoxed.

"What happens," said Graham, "is that I get in touch with colleagues and explain the situation. I can find out who's itching for a new challenge, and who's concentrating on the Mississippian culture right now. Both Boston University and the University of Texas at Austin have excellent archaeology programs and might consider sponsoring the exploration."

"But the programs at the Lodge!" protested Mr. Roderick, alarmed.

Graham held out a cautionary hand. "This process will be slow and deliberate. It could span years, and discovery and exploration will impact the daily operations of the Lodge as little as possible. Take heart, Ken. I think this could be monumental for your organization as well as for academic discovery, if you let it."

"It sure is overwhelming, though," said Sean. "To think of what is beneath us, and what could be found!"

"Archaeology is like that," said Graham. "It seems the more you find, there is still more to uncover."

"What did you find in that doorway that startled you?" asked Chu.

Graham lost some of his calm. "It was the most astonishing thing. I got a clear picture on the GPR of a face mask!" he said. "It likely is covered in copper for the instrument to detect it so clearly. Face masks carved from cedar were found at the Etowah mounds here in Georgia and at the Emmons site in Illinois, and both of those were covered with or had traces of copper. This one almost leapt out of the computer display! I wasn't expecting something so definitive."

"It wasn't a head pot, though?" asked Emmett. Graham shook his head.

"What's a head pot?" asked Sean. "Is it like a face jug?"

"Actually, yes. It's a Mississippian pottery vessel, a whole head complete with ears and forehead decorations. Over a hundred were found at Mississippian sites in Arkansas, and only in Arkansas," explained Graham.

He looked at the storage room with a frown. "What a coincidence, to find that mask at the threshold of the room holding face jugs."

Lucie and Andrea exchanged glances.

"Can we see it?" asked Lucie brightly.

"Oh, I am so sorry!" said Graham. "Of course, you should all have a chance. It's remarkably clear." He turned on the power to the GPR and asked, "Who's first?"

16

A week passed, and Lucie finally got to spend Saturday morning at Andrea's. They made some awesome multi-media art, covering a square of canvas with tinted gesso, paper flowers, iridescent medium, and glitter. She had a few sore spots on her fingers because they'd been using a hot glue gun to connect the butterfly wings and flowers, and she didn't always aim well.

She was in Andrea's kitchen, searching in the first-aid kit for some antibiotic cream, when her mom came to pick her up.

"Hey, sweetie," said her mom, coming in from the living room door with Andrea's mom Serrie. "What happened?"

"Just some hot glue," said Lucie. "Look at my craft!" She pointed at her creation on the kitchen table as she dabbed at her spots with the cream.

"Wow!" said Laurel, bending over to get a good look. Andrea's little brother Patrick came zooming in from the living room holding a truck, bumped into Laurel's behind, and careened away.

"Ooof!" Laurel's breath left her body, her stomach hitting the table.

"Sorry! 'Scuse!" called the other twin, Alaina, who was close behind her brother, dark pigtails streaming behind her. She galloped after him and disappeared.

"Kids! Settle down!" exclaimed Serrie. "Laurel, are you okay? They always get wound up after lunch."

"Oh, sure," said Laurel, rubbing her midriff. "No harm done."

Andrea came in, holding her own creation. "Mom, can I put this on the table here? I don't want the twins to get at it."

"Won't it be safer in your room?" her mom asked.

"I guess," said Andrea reluctantly. "But they get in there sometimes, too." She started back out the door.

"Hey, Andrea, wait a minute," said Laurel. "The folks at the Crack-Stackin' Pottery fired some of my pieces last week in their kiln, and I haven't had the chance to pick them up. Would you like to come with Lucie and me now to get them?"

"Can I, Mom?" asked Andrea.

"I don't see why not," said Serrie. "I'd love to go back, too, but the twins would create more havoc than I'd like if we take them. Go ahead!"

The girls put away their craft supplies, found their shoes, and with some difficulty pulled Laurel away from talking to Serrie. The drive to the pottery was beautiful, because the leaves were finally turning stunning shades of blazing red, shimmering orange, and blinding yellow. They covered the mountains in a tapestry of color, warming the ancient hills with a quilted rainbow. Laurel's minivan crunched over the gravel leading from the main road, passing under a bower of trees bright in the sunlight.

The Crack-Stackin' Pottery was doing a brisk business this Saturday morning, and there was even a delivery van in the parking lot. Laurel and the girls got out of the minivan and headed into the store entrance.

Lucie blinked a little, her eyes getting used to the dimmer light inside. Her feet echoed over the wooden floors, and as her mom asked at the counter for Zimina, Lucie found herself wandering over to the museum. Andrea, who had stopped to check the price on a little owl, appeared at her elbow.

"Who would've thought what we'd find, the last time we were here?" she said softly to Lucie.

"I know!" said Lucie, gazing through the doorway at the pictures of the native mounds. "I still have trouble believing it."

Someone passed by them wheeling boxes on a handcart, headed to a display. "Carmen!" said Laurel's voice. "It's been so long!"

"Carmen?" said Lucie, looking quickly at Andrea. They scooted around customers in the aisles to get a good look. Sure enough, it was the frizzy-haired lady whose boxes they'd delivered at the Festival.

"It has been a time!" said Carmen, all smiles. "How are you Laurel? What brings you here?"

"I'm picking up some of my work. Zimina was kind enough to fire them for me," said Laurel. She noticed the girls watching. "Do you know my daughter, Lucie, and her friend, Andrea Longstreet?"

Carmen's forehead furrowed. "No, I don't think so," she said.

Andrea said, "We were helping at the Shuford Lodge Festival. We brought you some boxes."

"Oh, was that you?" said Carmen, her brow clearing. "What a day that was. I wasn't even supposed to be there. I've always tried my best to stay away from Shuford Lodge and usually send someone else."

"Send someone else where?" came Zimina's voice from behind the girls. She set a box on the store counter, avoiding the customers at the cash register. "Here, Laurel, this is the first box." She looked at Carmen. "Well?"

"Shuford Lodge. I hate going there; it's such bad luck," said Carmen.

"Not anymore!" said Zimina, wagging a finger at her. "You know why we thought that now."

"Well, yes," said Carmen reluctantly.

"I'm sorry," said Lucie. "You thought what about Shuford Lodge?"

"Our great-grandmothers were sisters," said Zimina, motioning to Carmen. "Their mother was a Native American, and she was a fearsome woman. She taught her children that the land around Shuford Lodge was full of ghosts, sadness, and bad karma, for the lack of a better word. It seeped down through the family, and we've avoided it all our lives. We call it the waya land, land of the wolf."

"But now," continued Carmen, "with the discovery of the native mound there, it changes everything! Have you heard about that?" she asked the girls.

"Yes, we have," they assured her, working to keep their faces straight.

"I can't believe it," said Carmen. "All those years, all that fear and worry, turns out to be just a story that got twisted."

"It's like the game of telephone," chuckled Zimina. "Words and meaning get garbled if you don't take care of them, creating a big mess."

"You know, maybe we weren't supposed to be afraid of wolves," said Carmen thoughtfully. "Maybe we were supposed to protect them."

Andera tilted her head. "Is that why you don't make anything with wolves here at the pottery? Because of the fear in your family?" she asked.

Zimina nodded. "I'll make sure that changes now, though. We shouldn't be afraid of things, because it's really people who create the fear, not things."

"Samma Tahe!" Lucie whispered, staring at Zimina.

"I'm sorry?" said Zimina.

Lucie blinked. "Sorry. It's just that I heard someone else say that not long ago."

Laurel put an arm around Lucie. "I'm glad the discovery at the Shuford Lodge was made," she told Carmen and Zimina. "The more we understand about the world and history, the better decisions we can make for the future."

"Amen to that," said Carmen with satisfaction.

"Absolutely!" echoed Zimina. "And on that note, let me get your next box. I'll come out the other door." She left the store, headed for the workroom.

Laurel picked up her box, and the girls followed her out of the store. As Laurel loaded the box in the minivan, Lucie thought she saw movement out of the corner of her eye, but when she turned to look, nothing was there.

Laurel went to meet Zimina at the workroom door, and Lucie started to drift toward the ravine holding the Crack-Stackin' Pottery pyramid. Again, she saw movement out of the corner of her eye, and as she turned her head, getting a clearer image, she heard Andrea yell, "Did you see that?"

Lucie's head whipped around to see Andrea take off running. She ran after her, down the ravine steps toward the pottery pyramid. The tinkling sounds from the water running through the pots was loud in her ears. Andrea suddenly stopped short, her breath coming fast and excited.

"Where did it go?" Andrea cried, her eyes searching the scene. "Did you see it?"

"I saw a little girl running," said Lucie, she too looking everywhere. "She was wearing a ruffled dress. Didn't you see her?"

"A little girl?" said Andrea, turning to look at Lucie, her cheeks flushed pink. "I didn't see any little girl. I saw a wolf."

Lucie stared at her. Goosebumps rose all along her arms, and her hair seemed to stand on end. "You saw a wolf?" she asked breathlessly.

"Yeah," insisted Andrea, her arms thrown wild with emphasis. "There was a big wolf, just running across the edge of the woods. It looked right at me, and then it ran down here. How could you miss it?"

Lucie put a hand out, gently touching Andrea's arm, trying to calm her. "You're of the wolf clan," she said.

"Yeah, so?" said Andrea loudly. "My dad's whole family is."

"So, our mystery was to save the heritage of the wolf people," explained Lucie. "You have a connection to them, and in my dream with Julianna, we were running, wild and free, through the mountains. If you'd had the same dream, you might not have seen Julianna; you might have seen a wolf running, wild and free."

It was Andrea's turn to stare. "You mean…"

"I think we just got a thank you, but each in the way we could understand," said Lucie gently. "I saw Julianna, who wanted so badly for her world to be kind and fair, and you saw something of the waya people, who needed to be respected and protected."

Andrea brought her hand up to grip Lucie's elbow. "We did do that, didn't we? In a small way, we made a difference."

They looked at each other for a long moment, and then, slipping arms around each other, dark and light heads touching, they started back up the hill. But as they reached the top, they turned as one to look once more at the surrounding, ancient mountains. They heard the watery music chime in the fountain, they saw the warm rainbow of the turning leaves, and they felt peace, peace envelope them both like a hug.

And then, on the breath of a breeze, with a hint of violin… it was gone.

THE END

Author's Notes

As for the people in the book who really walked this earth:

George Ann Hughes Hawthorne, the daughter of William Hughes and Frances Simpson, was born about May 1850, and in about 1866 she married Dr. Masterson Ogden Hawthorne. He was a physician in Ballard County, Kentucky, following in his own father William's footsteps. Masterson's first wife, Eva Bodkins Hawthorne, died sometime between 1860 and 1865, leaving two sons, Charlie and William.

Masterson died in December 1870, and the family seems to have broken up a few years later. A biography of Masterson and Eva's son Charlie mentions that at age fifteen (about 1873), he went to live with an uncle. While George Ann's children, Masterson Jr. (my great-great-grandfather, known as Bob) and Frances, are found living with her parents in the 1880 Ballard County Federal Census, we have no further records of George Ann, most likely due to the records fire in Ballard County in 1880.

Julianna Cameron Yongue was born in the year 1790, one of seven children born to Scottish immigrant James Cameron and his wife, Jennet Moore. In February 1807, she married Martin Yongue, son of Irish immigrant Samuel Yongue,

and nine children were born to Julianna and
Martin. Both the Cameron and Yongue families
settled in Fairfield District, South Carolina, and
both families owned slaves. Julianna, my husband's
3rd great-grandmother, died at the ripe old age of
84 in 1874, and she is buried in Salem Presbyterian
Church in Fairfield County, South Carolina.

Her father, James Cameron, served in the
Revolutionary War under Capt. Edward Martin in
Colonel Richard Winn's Regiment, both on
horseback and on foot. His will was recorded in
Fairfield District, South Carolina in 1831.

Johannes Jurian Westvaal was born about 1659
at Foxhall, the manor of Thomas Chambers, in
what is now Kingston, New York. His parents were
Jurian Juriansen Westvaal and Marretje Hansen,
both of whom were born in the Netherlands.

Jurian, Johannes's father, immigrated at the
age of thirteen to New Amsterdam in 1642 on the
ship *De Houttwyn*. After a time of indenture, he
became a free man at the age of twenty-one, and by
1654 he bought land in the Esopus region of New
York. He and Marretje Hansen were the parents of
six children, and Jurian is described in *A History of
Ontario County, New York and Its People*, by Charles F.
Milliken, as "a steady, persevering, upright and
influential citizen."

Relations with the natives in the Esopus
region were not smooth for the Dutch colonists.
Misunderstandings and rash decisions led to death

on both sides. A truce had been in place for several years before 1667, when Jurian served as guide for a party of English soldiers exploring the land. Jurian was hit by an arrow when their party was attacked by native warriors, and he did not survive.

Jurian's wife Marretje, widowed with six children to support, married Jacob Jansen before 1670, when she appears in court records explaining how he was unable to work their farm. She had at least one child with Jacob.

Jurian's close friend Captain Thomas Chambers was an instrumental figure in the foundation of Kingston, New York and was one of its earliest settlers. In the book *When Cultures Collide*, by Susan Stessin-Cohn, he is described as "an imposing figure: tall, lean and red headed. He was known to be a *prudent and thrifty businessman*," and the *New York Genealogical and Biographical Record*, Volume 33, (1902) names him as "one of the most energetic, influential and prosperous settlers at that place, and his valuable services on behalf of the Government were recognized by Governor Lovelace in 1672 by the creation of a manor out of his estate *to be known by ye name of ye Manor of ffox Hall*."

Johannes, Jurian's son, married Maritje Jacobz Cool in 1683, and they eventually raised their family of twelve children in Deerpark, Orange County, New York. Johannes did get himself in trouble, however. He drove a wagon, snapping his fingers, on the Sabbath, and was fined by the courts for such shocking behavior.

Westvaal family researchers have noted that Thomas Chambers remained a strongly influential person in Johannes's life after his father's death, and that Johannes's children had close relationships with the Munsee children, hunting, trapping, and trading with them. The graves of Johannes and Maritje, my 9th great-grandparents, are found in the Magagkamack Churchyard in Orange County.

Nathaniel Tatum and Nicholas Granger arrived in Virginia in May 1619 on the ship *George*, captained by William Ewen. Nathaniel is thought to have been about fifteen years old at the time. They were among a group of seventy-five boys and twenty-five girls, aged 8 to 16, who were taken off the streets of London and were housed in Bridewell Prison for a few months before the journey. Although several ships brought similar groups of children to Virginia, of them all, only two of those children can be traced as having left descendants. Their names were Nathaniel Tatum and Nicholas Granger.

Nathaniel, my 9th great-grandfather, made a return trip to England sometime before 1638, where it is apparent that he got married, but he returned to Virginia. In 1638 he was awarded 100 acres on the Appomattox River (in Virginia) for having funded the transportation from England of his wife Ann and daughter Mary. He died after

January 1675/76, when he gifted land to his grandson, Nathaniel Tatum.

Another of Nathaniel's grandsons, Christopher Tatum, married Bridget Scott, who was the great-granddaughter of Cheney Boyce, an Ancient Planter, member of the Virginia House of Burgesses, and my 10th great-grandfather. (An Ancient Planter is a person who came to Virginia before 1616, remained for three years, and paid his/her own way.)

Temperance Flowerdew Yeardley was also an Ancient Planter. She was the wife of George Yeardley, who served as Governor of Virginia from 1619-1621 as well as from 1626 to his death in 1627. She then married Francis West, Governor of Virginia from 1627-1629 and my 11th great-uncle. Temperance died in December 1628, leaving three children.

Jane McWhorter Brevard, mother of twelve, was born about 1716. Her parents, Dr. Hugh McWhorter and Jean Gillespie, were Scotch-Irish, and they followed the pattern of many families in the early 1700's of settling in a northern colony, in their case Maryland, and then migrating within a generation to North Carolina.

In Iredell County, North Carolina Jane married John Brevard, the son of Jean Brevard and Mary Katherine McKnitt. Mary Katherine's family was Scotch-Irish, like the McWhorters, but Jean Brevard was a French Huguenot, fleeing France for religious freedom. He and the McKnitts sailed together on the voyage to the New World, and Jean and Mary Katherine were married about 1712.

All these families were intensely involved in the American Revolution, fighting for the freedom of the colonies. Jane McWhorter Brevard's brother, minister Dr. Alexander McWhorter, was appointed by Congress to persuade the Royalists of North Carolina to the cause of freedom, and he was present at General Washington's crossing of the Delaware River in 1776. John Brevard's maternal relatives were the Alexanders, thirteen of whom signed the Mecklenburg Declaration of Independence, a document that predates the nation's Declaration of Independence. The Revolutionary service of John and Jane's son, Dr. Ephraim Brevard, was honored by the naming of Brevard, North Carolina for him.

John and Jane themselves are each listed by the Daughters of the American Revolution as having given Patriotic Service in North Carolina. All eight of their sons served in the Revolutionary Army, and their son-in-law, General William Lee Davidson, was killed by Tory (Loyalist) soldiers at the battle of Cowan's Ford in February 1781. His wife, Mary Brevard Davidson, left their seven children, one only a month old, to ride by horseback fifteen miles through enemy territory to his burial by torchlight at Hopewell Presbyterian Church.

Soon after, a band of Tories came to John and Jane's home, finding Jane alone, as she had sent her daughters to safety across the swamps. The Tories burned every building on the place. Account after account calls her "venerable matron," cites that the Tories told her "she had eight sons in the rebel army" as cause for the burning, mentions that she went back into the house time and time again to save furniture, and that the Tories threw everything back into the fire. Jane lived until May 25, 1800, and she is buried with her husband at Centre Presbyterian Church Cemetery in Iredell County, North Carolina. They were my 8th great-grandparents.

The Munsees were Native Americans who lived in the lower Hudson Valley and the upper Delaware River, in the Catskills Mountains. They were part of the Lenape people, who were divided into three groups: the Unami, which means "turtle," the Uchlato, which means "turkey," and the Minsi, or Munsee, which means "wolf." (http://www.angelfire.com/ny3/cmsvriverlovers/native.html) The Lenapes were members of the greater Delaware tribe, which itself was a division of the "Algonquians, which included eighty-four major nations and spanned the continent." (https://www.nytimes.com/2004/05/02/nyregion/in-their-footsteps.html) Europeans, both Dutch and English, called them "Esopus," since they lived along the Esopus River.

The Munsees traded with the Europeans, met with the Europeans on treaties, fought with the Europeans over disagreements and grievances, and eventually over the centuries were moved farther and farther west and north, ending up in Wisconsin and Canada. They lost much of their heritage, and it is only within the last few decades that they have begun reclaiming that knowledge.

The word "mpatamweikaonëna" that Nanichi uses when talking to Johannes means "temple, house of prayer."

My sources for Nanichi's language in Lucie's dream from Johannes Westvaal are several websites. One, http://talk-lenape.org, is an online Lenape talking dictionary based on work supported by the National Science Foundation. It can be searched by English or Lenape words, and it is compiled from the knowledge of native Lenape speakers.

Another site was http://www.bigorrin.org/archive23.htm, which based its data on work published by John O'Meara, *Delaware-English English-Delaware Dictionary*. Check out http://www.worldcat.org/advancedsearch to find a copy in a library near you. Mr. O'Meara, a Canadian linguist, studied the language and made extensive recordings in addition to several published works on the Delaware language.

While Nanichi is a name I created, it was based on the names of the Munsee chiefs who were involved in a treaty for Thomas Chambers's land grant in 1652. Kawachhikan and Sowappekat signed the treaty and stated that they were empowered by others, namely Nachomaet, Kranachkoos, Pronapa, Siaranich, Sikamach, Awardaris, Quanachha, and Warikappano, to grant the land.

A publication by the Ulster County Clerk's Office, *When Cultures Collide* by Susan Stessin-Cohn and Lucian Valdiva, available in PDF at http://ulstercountyny.gov/archives/downloads/cultures/When_Cultures_Collide-Full.pdf, is a wonderful teaching resource for exploring the Munsees (Esopus) and their interactions with the Europeans.

I will give my love an apple is an ancient riddle song from the British Isles, dating back to the 15th century. A particularly beautiful version by Iona can be found on YouTube.

Paw Paw Patch is a children's song about a fruit native to the Appalachian Mountains of North America. Paw paws are about the size and shape of a cucumber, and they are apparently quite tasty and full of nutrients.

I found the name Samma Tahe on the 1835 Henderson Rolls in Georgia, a census taken of the Cherokee living in Alabama, Georgia, Tennessee, and North Carolina prior to the Trail of Tears.

Pat Shields and Janice Hall of Georgia Mudcats Pottery use the term *playing with the dragon* in one of their face jug videos on YouTube, and I love how descriptive it is! Janice generously gave permission to include it in this book.

In 1971, the International Horn Society recommended at its first meeting that Horn (with a capital H) be recognized as the correct name for what was widely known as the French horn, since it is a German instrument, not a French one! My teacher Robert Pruzin, a former member of the President's Own Marine Band in Washington, D.C. impressed this fact upon me the moment I stepped foot on campus as a freshman at the University of South Carolina. As well, my Horn pedigree is also one step removed (through Dr. John Dressler) from Philip Farkas, one of the giants of the Horn world and a co-founder of the International Horn Society. Thus, Lucie plays a Horn with a capital H!

ACKNOWLEDGEMENTS

Once upon a time, there were two little girls who grew up the best of friends. They shared love of fun and books and music, spent long hours talking on the phone as teenagers, competed in classes, and could see in a split-second flash of the eyes what the other was thinking. Many of their classmates were from families that had lived in the area for generations, but these two girls had only their parents and siblings nearby.

They grew up, went to college, got engaged and married within five months of each other. Each served as bridesmaid in the other's wedding, and they met every so often over the years to catch up. Then one became entranced with genealogy, and through a chance "could you check out this name" from the other, discovered that those two girls were really cousins. Eight generations back, three hundred and fifty years back, they shared the same ancestors in New York. One friend's family moved west, ultimately to California, while the other's family migrated to North Carolina. And in a little town in Georgia, they came back together.

I am grateful for the friendship, the laughs, and the memories. From my heart to yours, Kim, thank you!

Many thanks to Lynn Westfall Kilpatrick, who took the Westvaal ball and followed it to New

York and then across the Atlantic to the Netherlands. Her hard work and findings provided the foundation of building the world of Jurian and Johannes, and I so appreciate her generosity in sharing them as well as her guidance!

My thanks as always go out to my first readers, Sandra and Charles Aiken, Joan Curtis, Betty Highsmith, and James and Katie Dickson. Your suggestions, edits, and insights have made the story richer and stronger!

I have a supportive, loving family as my center, and Jim, James, Katie, and Tanner *the schnauzer at my feet* make it so. My love to you—with chocolate-chip and butterscotch-chip cookies on top! *Well, except for Tanner. We'll find another treat!*

ABOUT THE AUTHOR

Born into a family of teachers, Jennifer Aiken Dickson followed the family tradition and taught music, band, and chorus for almost a decade before having her own children. Then one day her father told her he had always believed she could write children's books, and four months later, Lucie blossomed into her mind. Set in the Northeast Georgia Mountains of her childhood, flavored with the love for her family, genealogy, and possibilities, Lucie and Andrea's adventures brought Jennifer's dreams to life. Follow Jennifer on Twitter (@luciebrandonbks) or reach her at luciebrandonmysteries@gmail.com.

Made in the USA
Middletown, DE
23 February 2019